Standoff
at Sunrise
Creek

Crossway Books by
STEPHEN BLY

THE STUART BRANNON WESTERN SERIES
Hard Winter at Broken Arrow Crossing
False Claims at the Little Stephen Mine
Last Hanging at Paradise Meadow
Standoff at Sunrise Creek

THE NATHAN T. RIGGINS WESTERN ADVENTURE SERIES (AGES 9–14)
The Dog Who Would Not Smile
Coyote True
You Can Always Trust a Spotted Horse

Standoff at Sunrise Creek

Stephen Bly

CROSSWAY BOOKS • WHEATON, ILLINOIS
A DIVISION OF GOOD NEWS PUBLISHERS

Standoff at Sunrise Creek.

Copyright © 1993 by Stephen Bly.

Published by Crossway Books, a division of Good News Publishers, 1300 Crescent Street, Wheaton, Illinois 60187.

Cover illustration: Den Schofield

First printing, 1993

Printed in the United States of America

Library of Congress Cataloging-in-Publication Data
Bly, Stephen A., 1944-
    Standoff at Sunrise Creek / Stephen Bly.
      p.   cm. — (The Stuart Brannon western adventure series)
    I. Title.   II. Series: Bly, Stephen A., 1944-   Stuart Brannon
western adventure series.
PS3552.L93S7 1993   813'.54—dc20   92-33517
ISBN 0-89107-695-6   *7.99/4.79 Ingram*

01		00		99		98		97		96		95		94		93
15	14	13	12	11	10	9	8	7	6	5	4	3	2	1

5-1-97

For a list of other books by
Stephen Bly
or information regarding speaking engagements
write:
Stephen Bly
Winchester, Idaho 83555

For
MARK *and* JAYNE
living
on the
frontier

ONE

It sounded like the echo of a distant rifle.
Just a single shot.
Then the howl of the wind.

Brannon wasn't sure. He hated to pull his Winchester out of the scabbard. He hoped to protect it from the sandstorm. But in this case, precaution outweighed a clean barrel.

Stuart Brannon had no idea where Ute country ended and Navajo country began. He didn't know whether he was in Utah, Arizona, or even still in New Mexico Territory. Somewhere up to the north he expected to find the San Juan River, and somewhere down below should be Mexican Water.

A bitter, hot wind raged out of the canyons to the west and swirled across the flat, parched desert floor. There was no clean air to breathe. No peaceful vistas to view. His black hat was tied on and pulled down, his red bandanna yanked up over his nose.

His eyes reduced to narrow slits, horizontal gun slots in a fortress wall. Fine dust sucked his tongue dry and ground like flour on a millstone between his teeth. He could feel the rough cotton shirt grit the dirt into his shoulders. The heat of the sand inside his boots pained his raw feet.

When he could see anything at all, only small scattered gray sagebrush came into view.

Again, sounding even more distant, came the report of a rifle. He jerked the reins tight and stood in the stirrups.

No horizon.

No signs of life.

Brannon had known when he started the trip this wasn't the main road to Arizona. "It's the Old Spanish Trail," friends at Tres Casas advised. "It will cut three days off the trip . . . if you survive!"

He had every intention of surviving, but now he doubted the cost of saving those three days. He had spent the winter sheriff-ing in New Mexico . . . shot his way out of Paradise Meadow, and lingered one last week in Tres Casas.

On Monday Brannon had said good-bye to the Shepherds, Mulroneys, and Rose Creek and headed southwest. It was now Friday . . . or maybe Saturday. He wasn't sure.

He glanced down at El Viento. The horse's eyes were shut.

Oh, sure, you can keep 'em closed! As long as one of us knows where we're going. That Old Spanish Trail is around here some-place. Probably over by that rifle fire.

Brannon figured there were three things a man could do when he heard the sound of shooting. He could ride away from it . . . he could ride straight into it . . . or he could keep on the trail and try to ignore it.

He'd have chosen the last, but since he was not at all sure where the trail was, he turned the big black gelding directly into the wind and trotted in the direction of the gunfire.

Approaching what looked through the dust to be the head of a wash, Brannon dismounted and led El Viento towards the precipice. As he expected, the wind galed at the crest. Yet vision improved.

A mesa? We've been up on a mesa? Well, old boy, it's a good thing we didn't plow on over the side!

As the dust and sand circled around him, he thought he could see a ribbon of green on the desert floor below. He believed he could observe several horses at a bend in the greenery.

Or perhaps they were just dark boulders. . . .

He knew for sure that he heard two more shots.

There was no quick way down off the mesa. To plummet off the edge would be suicide—either by the fall or perhaps by the guns that waited below.

It will take me half an hour to work my way around to the south and back up that river!

Knowing it was his only reasonable choice, Brannon turned El Viento south and loped the horse through the roaring sandstorm. As he worked his way off the south end of the mesa, the wind decreased the more he descended.

He found that vision improved on the valley floor, which allowed him to see a row of brush sheltering a stream or, at least, a stream bed. Brannon held El Viento back against the base of the mesa and waited for another gunshot to reveal position.

He pulled his canteen off the saddle, sloshed some water into his cupped hand, and let the horse slobber up the moisture. Then he took a swig out of the canteen and pulled off his bandanna. Soaking the red rag, he wiped off his face, wrung it out, and retied it around his neck.

Maybe just some target practice . . . or shooting at game, but I can't imagine what game there would be out here. If those were horses I sighted, and if they are the only ones out here, and if they haven't moved, and if they are just pilgrims passing through, then . . .

Brannon shoved a few more shells into the breech of the Winchester. Then he dug his extra Colt out of the bedroll tied to the cantle, spun the chamber, and jammed the gun into his belt.

I've been wrong before.

He adjusted the cinch on El Viento, remounted, and rode out away from the mesa toward what he supposed to be a river. The green ribbon he had spotted from on top turned out to be brush, not trees, and what he hoped was a river was only a meager creek, already starting to sink back into its underground summer resting place.

As El Viento drank his fill, Brannon slipped down out of the saddle and filled his canteen, never releasing his grip on the Winchester nor taking his eyes off the north. He spied a rough trail on the far side of the creek.

No reason to be too obvious. Come on, boy. We'll stay over in this brush.

The wind was so mild that the dust storm now looked merely

like clouds up on the mesa. As Brannon rode straight into the breeze, he noticed El Viento twitch his ears.

He pulled up on the reins and turned his head.

"What do you hear, boy?" he whispered.

Then, in the hum of the breeze, they both heard the whinny of a horse.

"Well, someone's up there!"

Fearing making too high a profile above the brush, Brannon dismounted and led El Viento towards the sound of the horse. Walking slowly and quietly, he edged his way closer until he heard not only a horse, but jumbled voices shouting.

Someone's not exactly happy.

Brannon caught sight of a wagon and team. Four saddled horses milled around near the wagon, but no one was in sight. Tying off El Viento, he crept through the head-high brush until he could see into a slight clearing next to the creek.

Still unable to distinguish the voices, he could see several men with guns pointed towards a dark-haired twosome huddled in the middle of a circle.

The gunmen looked dirty . . . rough . . . hard . . . the kind that drifted into most every western town—men who would end up as early residents of Boot Hill or the guests of honor at a necktie party.

Well, Brannon . . . how can you take sides when you don't know the argument? Looks like a man's down . . . maybe two. Mexicans . . . and a woman!

Glancing at the man and woman, he recognized the dark satin and lace, the waist-length jacket, and the tall stove-top boots of Mexican aristocracy.

He cocked the lever on his Winchester as slowly as possible and inched his way closer. Now the voices were distinguishable.

"Sure hope you folks enjoy your new place! Right, Lacey?" a fat man in a brown vest sneered.

"Are we gonna leave 'em out here, Case?"

"Why, certainly. They wanted to see their rancho, and we showed it to them."

"Even the woman? We could take her with us, couldn't we?"

A younger man with a wispy beard stepped toward the couple. *Four horses . . . four men . . . four guns . . . maybe.*

Brannon was still trying to assess strategy when the youngest gunman reached out and grabbed the woman by the arm. Instantly, the man by her side threw a hard right into the jaw of the attacker, who then staggered back and tripped, sprawling into the sand.

With that action, one of those holding rifles cracked the barrel against the chivalrous Mexican's head. He crumpled to the ground near the feet of the woman, who screamed and bent down to cradle him.

Brannon froze as he saw the man lift the rifle to strike the woman. Then as if watching himself from a distance, he stepped out into the clearing and shouted, "Drop it, Mister!"

Startled, the man spun towards Brannon and lowered his barrel to fire.

He was too late.

The bullet from Brannon's Winchester slammed into the man's left shoulder, spun him around, and tumbled him into the middle of the creek.

"Holster those guns, boys, or you'll be stacked up like cordwood!"

"You can't fight all three of us!"

"That depends on how many friends I've got standing back in the brush."

"I don't see nobody!"

"Well, if you think I'm fool enough to ride out in this country by myself, then make a play. I don't know how good you are with those Colts, but you certainly know what I can do with this Winchester."

All three men held their weapons. The wounded fat man named Case struggled to pull himself out of the creek.

"Now, Mister, there ain't no reason for anyone else to get shot," the dirtiest of them said. "These Mexicans jumped us on the trail and we was defending ourselves. You ain't standin' up for no thievin' Mexicans, is ya?"

"What in the world did you have that they wanted?"

"Title to the property. From the New Mexico line to the Little Colorado!"

The three men began to spread themselves apart.

"You know, it's funny you boys should start wandering away from each other. That'll make me choose which one to shoot first. I believe your name is Lacey?" He motioned to the young man who had grabbed the woman. "Well, you'll be getting this .44 slug somewhere between the belt and the top of your head. Or you might convince these boys to stand still."

"You ain't got no help in the bushes or they'd have showed themselves by now," Lacey taunted. Turning his back to Brannon, he waved his dirty hat at the bush, "Go ahead, hombres! Shoot! Shoot!"

Suddenly a rifle fired from deep in the brush. The man's ripped hat flew into the creek. All three men instantly dropped their revolvers and threw their hands into the air.

Brannon glanced back over his shoulder and thought he spotted a flash of red.

"Call 'em off! Call 'em off!" Lacy pleaded.

"Oh, I don't tell another man how to shoot. If they want to kill you, I reckon they'll kill you."

Then, turning to the woman, he nodded. "¿Señora, como está este hombre? ¿Es su esposo?"

"Yes, he is my husband. I do not believe he is hurt very badly. Do you speak Spanish?"

"Not as well as you speak English," Brannon answered, never taking his eyes off the gunmen. "What happened here?"

"It is a very long story."

"They brought you out into the desert and tried to bushwhack you, I presume?"

"Yes, I believe that is correct."

"Do you have any food in the wagon?"

"We have a few supplies. Why?"

"Would you be able to leave your husband for a minute? I'll watch him if you could toss some food into a sack and bring it over here."

Then turning to the men, he ordered, "You three sit down back to back. Drag your *compadre* in there too."

"You ain't going to shoot us, are ya?"

"Nope."

The woman returned from the wagon with a few supplies.

"Can you hold this gun on them while I tie them up?"

"Yes . . . if I can control my anger long enough not to shoot them."

Glancing at the men, Brannon nodded. "Well, if you have to shoot one, shoot Lacey!"

"Mister, don't give that lousy Mexican a gun. Why, she'll—"

A doubled fist slammed into the man's midsection.

"Excuse me." Brannon pulled the man back up to a standing position and doubled his fist again. "Exactly what did you call this lady?"

Choking out a response, the man mumbled, "Señorita . . . Señorita!"

"Well, that's close enough."

Brannon tied the four men back to back, propping the wounded man with the others.

"What do we do now?" she asked.

"Is the other man dead?"

"Yes, I believe so. He is Enrique, our driver. A very courageous man."

"We'll load you folks in that wagon and roll on out of here. Where did you come from?"

"Prescott."

"Good. That's where I'm heading. Mind if I ride along?"

"I would be most grateful." She nodded. "Are you leaving the provisions for these *hombres malo?*"

"Nope. They don't deserve a thing. The food is for the Indians in the brush."

"Your assistants are Indians?" she quizzed.

"Not my assistants . . . just friends."

"Mister, you cain't leave us to the Injuns!"

Brannon ignored his plea.

"Red Shirt!" he called out. "I left some grub here. Will you see that these men do not leave for three days?"

"And after that?" a deep, slow voice shouted back.

"Let them go . . . or," he glanced at the men, "or eat them!"

"That is good!" the voice called back. "Is the Brannon going to Arizona?"

"Yep!"

"Brannon?" one of the men choked. "We were going up against Stuart Brannon?"

"Chalco asks when will you be coming back to our camp?" the still unseen Red Shirt called.

"Whenever I need your help. How is Chalco's leg?"

"It is well . . . and ugly like the rest of him," Red Shirt added.

"Hey, Mr. Brannon!" one of the bound men shouted. "We didn't know it was you!"

"And when will you and the others be coming to my camp in Arizona?" Brannon hollered to Red Shirt.

"When we need your help," came the reply.

"It is well," Brannon called.

Brannon helped the Mexican, now conscious, to the wagon. Then he retrieved the dead man.

"Brannon, you're not playing square!" one of the men called.

"Look, if I hadn't rode into camp, you would have killed these folks, mounted up, rode about ten feet, and been shot in the head by these Indians. Now they happen to owe me a favor, and they can't shoot you . . . unless you try to run away. I figure I saved your lives. At least for three days."

"What kind of Injuns are they? They ain't 'Paches, are they?"

"They're Ute. And quite friendly as long as they have plenty to eat. Look at it this way. You have at least three days to settle up with the Almighty."

Brannon hoisted the body across his shoulders and tramped back to the wagon. The Mexican woman was trying to tie a white bandage around her husband's head while holding the reins of the team in one hand. Brannon laid the body in the far back of the wagon and wrapped it with a canvas tarp that had been covering an ornate wooden trunk. He tied off El Viento to the tailgate of the wagon and climbed up next to the couple.

"You look like you need to rest, *amigo*. I can drive this thing if you'd like."

"*Gracias, Señor, gracias,*" the man mumbled and glanced over at his wife.

"*Es bueno, Don Rinaldo . . . es bueno!*" she murmured.

The man immediately crawled into the back of the wagon to lie down. Brannon slapped the reins, and the team bolted forward.

He turned to the woman and nodded. "Now just who are you folks and how did you get in such a bind?"

He studied her. Although slightly dusty and crumpled from her recent ordeal, she presented a fine portrait of a Mexican lady. *Twenty-eight to thirty. Thin. Maybe a little too thin. Long black dress with delicate embroidery work and beautiful lace . . . black hair pulled back behind her head with tortoise shell comb still in place . . . fiery brown eyes that controlled destinies with a glance.*

Suddenly he realized she had begun to speak.

" . . . and I know quite a little about you, Mr. Stuart Brannon."

"You do? Well . . . what have you heard?"

"Some say that you are a vicious, reckless gunman who hates Mexicans."

"What?"

"Yes."

"Who told you that?"

"This was told to me by a young man named Ramon Fuente-Delgado."

"Delgado? You mean the kid with the silver saddle and a bad choice of friends over in Tres Casas?"

"Yes, he said you did not treat him well."

"Oh, I don't know. He helped spring two men from my jail, broke into a saloon, tore up half the furnishings in the place, and cut me in the back with his knife. I believe I treated him pretty square."

"Yes." She began to smile. "I believe you did."

"Where did you run across Delgado?"

"Just outside the MacGruder ranch a few days ago."

"So he's in Arizona?"

"He's probably back in Mexico by now. He did not like your welcome."

"I presume he told you the other three I chased out of town were white?"

"You do not need to apologize to me," she continued. "Ramon is a very headstrong young man. I think he goes home wiser now."

"Do you know him well?"

"Oh, yes," she said smiling. "He's my brother."

Brannon sighed. "Well, I guess you did hear an earful."

"Yes, I did. And I also heard about you from—"

Her husband sat up in the back of the wagon, spoke to her in Spanish, and then laid back down.

"Don Rinaldo says we must thank you twice—first for spanking Ramon and now for saving us from the thieves."

"Well, you know something about me, but I still haven't heard *your* story." Brannon turned the team onto wagon ruts running due west into the breeze. The wind continued stiff, but the sand was no longer blowing, and visibility remained good.

"My name is Victoria Maria Alezon Fuentes-Delgado Pacifica, and this is my husband, Don Rinaldo. We live on our family estate at the base of the Sierra Madres, southeast of Magdalena. Originally, I came from Monterrey."

"Where your father is the *Alcalde*?"

"The Vice-Generale," she corrected. "Well, last fall after the, how do you say it, roundup—"

"You raise cattle?"

"Oh, yes. In the fall an American lawyer came to visit us at the rancho. His name was William Gitt and he—"

"Spanish Land Grant Gitt? Last I heard he got run out of the country."

"Ah . . . you know Mr. Gitt?"

"Nope. Just heard a few things about him, that's all."

"It doesn't sound encouraging," she said sighing.

"Continue, please."

"Well, Mr. Gitt, who speaks quite fluent Spanish, was returning to the States after doing extensive research in Guadalajara and

Mexico City. He had purchased a Spanish land grant in St. Louis and was trying to verify it from old colonial records.

"After several weeks of investigation, he could not find the papers that proved the grant, but he did discover many old documents supporting an Alezon land grant made to my great-grandfather by the governor of New Mexico at that time. As you probably know, those grants were upheld by the 1847 Treaty of Guadalupe Hidalgo."

"If they can be proved," Brannon added.

"Correct." She nodded. "Well, Gitt had a trunk load (that is it in the wagon) of documents and certified copies proving our claim."

"Why did he take them?"

"He told us that if he could not locate an heir, he was going to make a claim to the grant himself, the evidence being so strong. But since he located me, he wanted to sell us the documents so that he might pay for his expenses for all the research."

"So Gitt sold you a trunk load of documents?"

"Yes, but the price was not exorbitant, and we felt it would be worth investigation since we knew that Great-Grandfather Alezon spent much time in New Mexico—or Arizona as it is now called—digging for gold."

"And you came to investigate the land?"

"Yes, we waited until spring and then traveled north. We stopped in Tucson and showed our papers to the Surveyor-General and in Prescott to the Superintendent of Lands."

Brannon cradled his Winchester in his lap with his right hand and kept glancing behind the wagon. "And what was their conclusion?"

"Actually, they were quite pleasant, but they could tell us nothing. They had never heard of the Alezon grant, and they were not allowed to comment on the documents until these were officially presented to the Surveyor-General. But several of the documents stated that an Initial Monument marked the boundary of the grant, and people at the Land Office said that our claim would be much substantiated if we located that original marker."

Brannon glanced down at the dust and dirt caked to his duckings and wished that he could broom them off. "That's why you're here?"

"Correct. We brought three men with us from the rancho. Two of them decided they would abandon us for the gold diggings of Prescott. Enrique encouraged us to come on out here on our own. We had no idea exactly where to search. But we determined to find the marker for ourselves. However, yesterday at Aqua Amargo, we met Mr. Case and his friends, who assured us they had seen the monument and would lead us to it."

"For a price, no doubt." Brannon popped the reins on the lead horse's rump as they started up an incline.

"Yes . . . for one hundred dollars."

"Let me guess the rest. So you rode two days out here only to find your guides now wanted to rob you. Your driver got shot in the scuffle that followed, and I drifted down in the middle of the confrontation."

"*Mas o menos,* that is correct."

"If this doesn't sound too personal, why does some rich hacienda owner want to come all the way up to this wild country anyway?"

"I have been asking my Don Rinaldo that question for several weeks."

"And what does he say?"

"Things are not stable in our country. Generale Diaz rules harshly, and no one can stop him. My husband fears the day will come when the military confiscates all that we have worked for."

"So a place in the States could be an escape?"

"We thought it was worth the investigation."

"What do you think now?"

"It is not worth the life of another person." She glanced back at her husband. "I believe we should return home and forget about the land grant. But I will await Don Rinaldo's decision."

A dust devil slammed into the rig, and for a moment they stopped talking.

"Do you sell cows . . . or just your steers?" Brannon quizzed.

"We have many of both. Are you a cattleman as well as a gun-man?"

"I am only a cattleman—with a ranch and no cattle. I'd like to buy five hundred to a thousand head sometime during the next year. Could you supply that many?"

"It is my husband who operates the business," she replied. "But it would be an amount that we could supply. Where is your ranch?"

"Down towards the middle of Arizona, on a little stream we call Sunrise Creek."

For most of the afternoon they rolled along parallel to the brush, climbing slightly uphill towards some western mountains. At times the wind made all conversation impossible. But by the time the sun began to set, they climbed out of the desert floor, and the wind died.

The old trail followed a small tributary of the creek into the hills, and about halfway up the slope they discovered a tiny grassy meadow. A spring supplied a constant trickle of water.

Brannon pulled the wagon over and they made camp for the night.

By now Señor Pacifica had regained his strength and rode up front with his wife.

"You folks may certainly do whatever you'd like, but I suggest we bury your friend here. This desert heat is going to decay that body before we make it to Prescott. And if I were you two, I would sleep in the wagon tonight. What with snakes, scorpions, and tarantulas, this country doesn't make a real great bed."

"And you, Mr. Brannon . . . where will you camp?"

"By the fire. That should be safe enough."

Señor Pacifica spoke to his wife in Spanish. Then she turned to Brannon.

"My husband says that he does not wish to insult you, but he thinks it best if we all sleep with loaded guns."

"Tell him I would be insulted only if you didn't."

"Do you expect the evil men to return?"

"No, but this must be Navajo country . . . perhaps even Apache. Besides you don't know for sure what kind of man I am."

"Oh, I know." Señora Pacifica smiled.

"I could have fooled you. Your brother may be right."

"Well, we know more about you than I have revealed," she advised.

"Your brother told you more?"

"No. I believe you know Mr. Barton at the Land Office in Prescott?"

"I met him on the trail up in Colorado."

"Well, we had dinner with him, his wife, and a sister-in-law named Harriet Reed. She seems to know quite a bit about the legendary Stuart Brannon."

"Yes . . . well . . ." Brannon stammered. "I'll tend the horses and dig a grave for this brave *compadre*."

It was almost dark when Brannon laid the tarp-wrapped body in the hole. He looked down one last time, and then glanced at Mr. and Mrs. Pacifica.

"Say," he began, "I'm sorry there's no priest around, but if you folks would like to, you know, say a few words . . . or do something . . ."

Suddenly Señor Pacifica began to pray in Spanish, and as he did, the Señora translated into English. It was a long and fervent prayer concerning the unfailing mercy of God and the eternal saving power of the blood of Christ. Brannon stared at them long after they finished the prayer.

"Mr. Brannon?" she called.

"Yes, ma'am?"

"You look a little surprised."

"Well, I haven't heard many prayers in Spanish. That was beautiful."

"Did you assume we must have a priest to say our prayers?"

"Eh, no . . . well . . . I guess . . . I guess I just never thought about it much."

"Mr. Brannon, you would be quite shocked if you knew the whole story of Victoria Maria Alezon Fuentes-Delgado Pacifica."

TWO

If one sits for tea with her back to the window, facing the fireplace, it is easy to imagine being in Boston or Philadelphia. Provided, of course, you don't hear horrid curses or sporadic gunfire coming from the street.

Harriet Reed glanced up from the letter she was writing and noticed the lid tilted crooked on the green and white Chinese vase. She padded across the soft oriental rug to the mantle and seated the lid properly.

The ladies' drawing room near the street on the second floor of the Barton home was almost her exclusive domain. Every morning her sister Gwen would pop in for a quick visit, but the rest of the day the room was hers.

In the six months since they had moved to Prescott, Harriet perfected her regimen of reading, writing, and serving as hostess at the countless dinners Gwen and Nelson gave.

She spent most of her time indoors and only on occasion ventured down the hill to the shops and stores. Her work as chairman of the Library Organizing Committee brought her into contact with a few of the more prominent citizens, yet she still did not feel completely settled.

Sitting back down at the small cherrywood and leather writing table with brass lion paw feet, she continued to write.

It is a beautiful, wild, primitive country. It begs to be settled, tamed, broken. But it can be a lonely place. Gwendolyn has Nelson and, so she says, by Christmas their first child. If you would only move out, we could—oh, there I go. Of course you must stay, I know, I know.

You will write back and say if only I had married Curtis Terrington. Well, as you know, Mr. Terrington bores me to tears, and I certainly refuse to sentence myself to such a life.

As I suspected, the Territory of Arizona is anything but boring. Yet I've had ample time to work on my novel. No, you cannot read any of it yet, but of course, I'll send you a copy when it's finished.

Did I tell you that even the church services are quite different out here? Not nearly so rigid and formal. Respectful, mind you, but highly reflective of the casual lifestyle. The choir does quite well for being so small. All except Lilian DuShey. She is simply horrid. A screeching soprano that reminds me of Esther. (Forgive me, I shouldn't have said that!)

You asked about Mr. Brannon. I hadn't realized that his name was being mentioned in the eastern newspapers. I didn't mean to sound as if I know him well, but I do expect him to come through soon. Several telegrams came to him at this address indicating we should hold them for his arrival, so I presume he is on his way. I do hope it's not today, for it's almost 11:00 A.M. and I haven't gone downstairs yet.

Tell your father you need some healthy western air and come see us. We have plenty of room, and it would be just like our school days.

Give my best to Rachel.

Affectionately yours,
Miss Harriet Reed

A light breeze rippled across her room from the half-open window. The white lace curtains fluttered like a swan starting to take flight, then settled neatly back into place, just like everything else in the room.

From her earliest memory Harriet Reed knew she would be a writer. She could not remember a day when the thought didn't dominate her mind. She would not write books of sugary poetry,

but solid, vivid, powerful statements in prose. Schooled on everything from *The Iliad and the Odyssey* to Dickens and Dumas, she
intended to compete with the best.

On her own terms.

She would not use a man's name.

She would never consent to any *nom de plume*.

And they would not ignore her.

Her work would demand recognition.

That required sacrifice. As she dressed for the warm spring day,
she wondered how high a price she was willing to pay.

"Harriet, you're obsessed with your writing!" they all scolded
her.

She took that as a compliment.

It would be the only way to succeed.

But today, for a few minutes, she glanced at the pine-covered
mountains surrounding town and thought about taking a long
buggy ride. She could feel the breeze in her face, the jostle of the
carriage, see the wild flowers and green hills, and sense the pres-
ence of a strong, rugged man at the reins riding next to her.

Not just any man, of course.

She had one in mind.

As she walked down the stairs, she carried a cloth carefully
dusting a dustless bannister. When she reached the bottom of the
stairs, she retreated to the kitchen just as a knock sounded at the
door.

The opaque leaded glass in the front door prevented her from
seeing who was on the front steps. Out of habit, she glanced at
her reflection in the hall mirror, brushed her dark brown hair
behind her ears, and opened the door.

A medium-built man with waistcoat buttoned at the top and a
soiled black hat greeted her.

"Excuse me, ma'am, I need to see the Superintendent of
Lands."

"Oh . . . yes," she said nodding, "Mr. Barton is at the office
today. It's located—"

"Madam," the man sighed, "if he were at the Land Office, I

wouldn't be here. I was told he would be here for dinner, and it is of utmost importance that I talk to him."

"Forgive me. I had forgotten it was so late. Yes, well . . . I believe that he and Mrs. Barton are dining with the mayor. I'm sure he'll be back to his—"

"Where are they eating?" the man demanded.

"I'm not sure of that. All I know is—"

"Look, this is extremely important," he insisted.

She noticed what looked like a smear of dirt above the man's left eyebrow, and she wondered how long it had been since he last washed his shirt. "Sir, I have given you all the information I have. Would you care to leave your name? I will inform Mr. Barton of your call."

"The name's Willing. Dr. Willing."

"Oh, my, is this a medical emergency?"

"It's more important than that, lady. It's a land claim emergency!" He turned on his heels and began to descend the front steps.

"I'm sorry you missed Mr. Barton," she called.

"I assure you, I will not miss him," he huffed. "It would have been helpful if he had let the hired help know where he is!"

The man dashed down the wooden sidewalk and crossed the wide dirty street. She walked out on the porch and glanced at the dust rag she still held in her hand.

Hired help? Mistaken for a cleaning lady?

She looked down at her pale hands and long, thin, ringless fingers. Then peering into the street and the bright sunlit noonday, she thought she saw a man riding north on a tall, black horse. Ducking back inside the house, she glanced out the front window with intentions to trace the movement of the black horse. Instead, she noticed a small cobweb in the upper right-hand corner of the window. Immediately she scurried towards the hall closet to look for the feather duster.

It took four hard days for Brannon and Señor and Señora Pacifica to reach the base of the San Francisco peaks. They camped near McMillan's old corrals, next to Flagpole Springs. The next day, south of the Springs they came across a rough wagon road that had been hacked out by General George Crook and men a few years before. It led down the mountain to Camp Verde and then on south across the desert to Tucson.

The Pacificas decided to bypass Prescott and return home through Camp Verde, Tucson, and Magdalena.

"Señor Brannon, we both have greatly appreciated your assistance through this beautiful and frightening land. Our home will always be open to you."

"And I'm serious about buying those cattle. I'll write to you this summer and make arrangements."

"Yes, we will look forward to it. Please give our regards to Mr. and Mrs. Barton . . . and also Miss Reed." The woman studied his face one last time.

Brannon tipped his hat and turned west towards Prescott. As he loped down the rutted trail, he became increasingly aware that there were absolutely no other travelers.

No freight wagons.

No military contingents.

No drifters.

No pilgrims.

No prospectors.

No one.

Either a bridge is out . . . or Prescott is under siege . . . or the Apaches have left the reservation! Why did they send the general north? George Crook's the only man in the country that can tame them. Too successful, I guess . . . send him up for Crazy Horse and Sitting Bull. Everyone in the Territory knows they should have made him governor . . . everyone except whiskey drummers and crooked Indian agents.

Brannon rode El Viento off the trail and into the trees that lined the north side of the road. The vegetation changed from forest to chaparral.

'Course I could be wrong. Maybe nobody's traveling today. Sure, Brannon, they just decided to stay home and plant potatoes and corn!

He rode to the top of a knoll and surveyed the horizon. Straight west he could see some smoke among the greasewood and scrub oaks. With the wind at his back, he stayed off the wagon road and circled north of the smoke. Brannon figured he was three or four miles north of the smoke when he finally made it downwind enough to distinguish sporadic gunfire. He sat and listened.

It's a standoff . . . or one side is pinned down and the others are just waiting. They're saving bullets for something. If I keep to the trees, then down the row of oaks . . . maybe . . . just maybe I'll be able to sight them.

Brannon didn't locate a trail that would bypass the confrontation. He didn't even think to look for one.

As he drew closer to the occasional rifle shots, he spotted unshod pony tracks in the reddish-brown, grassless soil.

OK, one side is Indian . . . but against whom? And why?

He tied El Viento to a stubby tree. Shoving all his extra cartridges into his coat pockets, he slipped his knife into his boot. Stalking from one tree to another, he approached the gunfire.

Apaches! They've got someone pinned down, but they sure aren't taking any chances. A man couldn't shoot them from even this angle.

He could spot Indian movement, but he wasn't close enough to count numbers. They scurried from location to location, firing few shots.

They're closing in! Whoever's pinned down is getting desperate! They're wasting their shells . . . scared to death, no doubt.

Brannon knew just how they felt.

Apaches just don't quit. They never quit. Either you kill them or they kill you . . . or they capture you and . . . He refused to even think about what would happen then.

I can't fight them single-handed—not that many. I'll have to scare them off . . . make them think I'm greater in number . . . or power . . . or by sheer terror.

"Lord, this would be a good time to have about a hundred soldiers from Whipple Barracks ride up the road."

He turned quickly to the right to glance at the western horizon. A blur, a shadow, a movement only steps behind him caused him to jerk his head back. Suddenly a rifle barrel crashed into his right arm. He dropped the Winchester. Stumbling backward, falling to the ground, he tugged at his Colt with his left hand and turned.

All he saw was the butt of a rifle jam into his stomach. He gasped for breath as the Colt fell to the ground. Doubled over with his shoulder almost on his knees, he yanked his knife from his boot and flailed wildly at the sound of a hammer cocking on the rifle.

Slicing through the attacker's arm caused the Indian to drop the weapon and scream. Brannon thought he heard gunfire in the distance.

Either they're shooting at me . . . or they're too busy to notice what's happening up here!

The Indian, clutching his bleeding arm against his chest, yanked a knife from his belt. He lunged at Brannon, who jumped back and sliced at the man as he tumbled forward. This time he gashed the other arm.

As the Indian clutched his new wound, Brannon landed a jaw-crunching roundhouse right. The Indian toppled to the ground, banged his head against a boulder and didn't move.

Brannon lunged for his weapons and searched the landscape for other attackers. The Indians all seemed to be occupied at the standoff down below.

They're moving in now. It's about over. Where did this old boy come from? He must have been back with the horses. What horses?

Brannon ran to the crest of the hill just to the east and spotted a dozen horses in the draw. Trotting, he dragged the unconscious Indian over to the little clearing and approached a tall paint pony.

If I were the chief, this would be my horse!

He shoved the Indian backwards into the saddle of the paint, and then lashed his wounded arms behind him, tied to the saddle horn. Brannon gagged the Indian with his bandanna and used the saddle strings to tie the man's legs to the stirrup. The Indian began to come to and labored to free his hands and feet.

Pulling down the *reata* that had served as a barrier for the horses, Brannon led the paint down the hill towards the gunfire.

He expected all the other horses to follow. He stopped a couple hundred feet above the shooting and suddenly slapped the paint on the rump with his hat.

The horses sprinted towards the Indians, who, still keeping their position, instantly turned their guns toward the herd. They froze when they saw their wounded friend lashed backwards to the lead horse.

It was the split second Brannon needed.

In six rapid, booming shots, he brought down six horses including the big paint. The Indians seized the remaining horses and fled to the east without firing a shot in Brannon's direction. One Indian pulled the wounded man free and urged him on foot down the wagon road.

"Ho! You in the rocks!" Brannon shouted. "I'm coming down!"

"You're a welcome sight," a man hollered back. "How many of ya are there?"

"Just me."

"One?"

"And how many are in the rocks?" Brannon called back.

"Six of us—but three are wounded real bad."

Brannon approached the rocks just as a tall, gray-haired man in a sergeant's uniform stood and walked towards him.

"Army?" Brannon questioned.

"From Whipple Barracks," the man responded. "I'm Sergeant Cloverdale. Where in the world did you learn that trick?"

"Backward in the saddle and shooting the horses?"

"Yeah."

"From the Chiricahua Apache south of Camp Bowie about four years ago. Only the poor man they strapped to the saddle had his face burnt off."

"Savages!"

"Yeah, and it's effective. I still have nightmares about it," Brannon added. "You got your horses?"

"Yeah, but I don't think the men can ride."

"They don't have any choice. Load 'em up. I'll grab my pony and we'll head back to the barracks as fast as we dare."

"I didn't catch your name, Mister," the sergeant yelled.

"Brannon," he replied as he ran back up the hill.

At best a ten-minute lead . . . they'll be back . . . back to gather their gear off these dead horses . . . back to retaliate . . . back to make someone pay!

He spurred El Viento towards the roadway and the soldiers who were trying to pack their wounded colleagues into the saddles.

"Ain't no use . . ." the one with the severe stomach wound gasped. "I cain't ride."

"Mister," Brannon shouted, "in ten minutes those Apaches will be back here, and God help the man they find alive! The only chance you've got is to make it back to a doc."

"The ride will kill me," the man groaned.

"It's not the worst thing that can happen," Brannon barked.

"And I say we just hole up here and fight 'em off! There ain't no more than a dozen of 'em."

Sergeant Cloverdale grabbed the man by the hips and shoved him on up into the saddle. "Taylor, that's Stuart Brannon you're talkin' to!"

"Brannon? You . . . you're Stuart Brannon?"

"Have we met before?"

"Eh . . . no sir! I just heard . . . you know how folks talk. It's just that people have said, well, I never thought I'd meet you. I should have known no one else would take 'em on single-handed like that."

Brannon turned to Cloverdale, who was now mounted. "Sergeant, you're in command of these troops, and if it seems correct, you take one healthy man with you up front. Me and the other man will bring up the drag, and we'll put the wounded men in the middle."

"You've got no argument from me, Mr. Brannon. Line up, men. Let's move out. We'll have to keep her at a trot as long as we can."

Two of the wounded men had lost a considerable amount of blood and were extremely weak as they bounced along. They clutched tightly to the horns of the McClellans and bounced in and out of consciousness.

Taylor broke out in a cold sweat and then, delirious from fever, began talking and singing incessantly.

Maxwelton's braes are bonnie, where early falls the dew,
And 'twas there that Annie Laurie gave me her promise true;
Gave me her promise true, which ne'er forgot will be,
And for bonnie Annie Laurie, I'd lay me down and die.

Cloverdale brought the men to a halt, but the wounded man sang on.

"Taylor!" he shouted.

Brannon pulled up, stood in the stirrups to glance back down the road, and then pulled off his hat and ran a gloveless hand through his dark brown hair.

"Sergeant . . . let him sing!"

"The fever's making him delirious."

"I know," Brannon nodded, "but every man's got a right to a death song."

The sergeant stared at him for a minute. "You're right, Brannon. Even the Apaches have that right. I was with Major Brown in '72."

"At the cave in the Superstitions?"

"Yeah . . . I heard 'em singin'. Any man that doesn't stand in fear of Apache bravery is a fool!"

Brannon rode up alongside the singing man and managed to pull off Taylor's bandanna. He soaked it with water and then tied the wet rag around the fevered man's forehead.

"Sing it, Private. Sing it all!"

The man sang, cried, cursed, and hollered for the next fifteen minutes as they rode hard to the west.

"General Sheridan!" he cried. "I won't ride for Custer. He's a dog! Give me Crook, or at least Miles . . . but I won't ride for Custer!"

Her brow is like the snowdrift; her throat is like the swan;
Her face, it is the fairest that e'er the sun shone on;
That e'er . . .

The singing suddenly stopped. Brannon saw the man slump forward across the horse's neck and then tumble to the road. All the riders reined up. It was the sergeant who hit the ground first to check on the downed man.

Brannon knew the verdict even before Cloverdale nodded to the others and hoisted the dead man across the saddle. Once the body was laced on, they quickly resumed their journey.

It was Brannon who sang now, but soon all the men joined him.

That e'er the sun shone on; and dark blue is her eye,
And for bonnie Annie Laurie, I'd lay me down and die.
And for bonnie Annie Laurie, I'd lay me down and die.

The trip was quiet and uneventful for the rest of the day and on into the night. They didn't even consider stopping. The wounded men held on, and the others spoke little. At dawn they came to a creek crossing in a small valley, and they stopped to rest the horses.

"Brannon, I'm sending Houghton on into Whipple to get an ambulance wagon headed this way. I'm gambling that twelve Indians on six horses won't follow us now."

Brannon took a flat stick and began to rub the sweat off El Viento.

"I believe you're right, Sergeant," he said nodding. "How are your men?"

"Looks like we'll get them home, thanks to you."

"I'm mighty glad it worked. I really didn't have a backup plan."

"Well, it was our luck."

"Or Providence," Brannon added.

"You saying that it was the Almighty's doin's?"

Brannon resat his saddle. "What I'm saying is that everything is the Lord's doin's."

It wasn't until late that day when he actually caught sight of a column of troops and an ambulance wagon that Stuart Brannon began to relax. He waited for Sergeant Cloverdale to finish loading the wounded men in the wagon.

"Mr. Brannon, you in a hurry to go into Prescott?"

"Yep."

"Hate to imposition you, but I'd appreciate if you could stop by the barracks and give your account of the attack to the captain. It might help us to identify which band that was."

"That sounds reasonable. Can you check and see if a civilian can use your wire to send a telegraph?"

"That's a guarantee. Say, Brannon," the sergeant continued, "the men and I would be honored to buy you a round of the best whiskey in Prescott."

Brannon pushed back his black hat and grinned. "Sergeant, you make that a big, thick steak dinner and you've got yourself a deal."

"Don't drink, huh? Just like ol' man Crook."

"But," Brannon said with a laugh, "I don't ride a mule!"

"You're right about that. You got one of the finest looking ponies in the Territory. You weren't planning on running him in the Fourth of July races, were ya?"

"Not likely." Brannon laughed. Then he remounted and spurred El Viento on down the road.

The sight of men sprinting to the corrals and hurried shouts of command greeted Brannon and the others as they entered Whipple Barracks. He could see a contingent of about one hundred men preparing hurriedly to leave. He started to question the sergeant about the advisability of beginning pursuit only a hour or so before sunset, but he held back. Instead, he followed the sergeant up to the headquarters.

"Mr. Brannon, let the private take your horse and rub him down."

"Thank ya. I appreciate it." Then turning to the private, he asked, "If you could . . . do you mind graining him? Not too much now. If he gets really wound up, he won't stop running until we get to Florence. I'll pay for the grain."

"Oh, no, sir," the private replied. "There won't be any cost, no sir!"

"Thanks."

"Mr. Brannon," the young man continued, "I heard about what you did down on San Simon Creek . . . and I heard about what you did over in New Mexico and Colorado . . . and, well, I just never thought I'd get to meet you. Yes, sir, I'm mighty proud to make your acquaintance!" He vigorously shook Brannon's hand.

It wasn't the last hand he shook.

After giving his report to Captain Wells and politely declining an offer to ride out as a scout with the departing battalion, Brannon followed Cloverdale to the telegraph office. A group of soldiers huddled on the porch as they approached.

"That's him right there!" one of them pointed.

"That ain't him . . . Brannon's an old man."

"Maybe that's his son. I heard Stuart Brannon died years ago."

The sergeant cleared his throat. "Men! You look like school-girls waiting to go to the dance. Now shake hands with my friend, Stuart Brannon, and then get back to your barracks!"

Inside the office Brannon spoke briefly to the telegraph opera-tor. "I want you to send a message to Camp Verde. Tell them that a dozen Apaches will be drifting back down that way. One of them has a deep slash on each arm. They won't attack the camp, but they will steal some horses and shoot up some settlers if they can. Also, ask them if a Mexican couple, Señor and Señora Pacifica, have passed through. I'd hate to have those Apaches catch up with them."

When he stepped back outside the office, the only person there was the private who was returning El Viento.

"Thanks for taking care of him." Brannon nodded.

"If you ever wanted to sell that horse . . . I'd sell my soul to buy him."

"That soul of yours has already been bought, son," Brannon corrected.

"What?"

"Next time you're sitting in the barracks killin' time, take a look at the Bible story. It cost God a lot more than a good horse for that soul of yours! So don't go selling it out too cheap."

"Yes, sir. . . ." the young man stammered.

"Mr. Brannon," the sergeant interrupted, "the men who came in with us said they wanted to meet you in Prescott at the Lucky Dollar and buy you that steak dinner."

"Sounds fair enough. What time?"

"Nine o'clock. Will that work?"

"I'll be there." Brannon mounted and tipped his hat to the sergeant and the private.

The private saluted back.

Son? Did you hear that, Lisa? Am I getting that old?

At the thought of her name he reached back into his maleta, dug to the bottom of the bag, and clutched a small gold locket. Then he flipped open the lid with his thumb and held it so the evening light reflected on the small smiling face.

I'm on my way home, babe. I'm on my way home.

THREE

Prescott always reminded Brannon of a New England oasis—white clapboard Victorian houses with tall rows of steps and big front porches. The old Spanish southwest design had been purposely avoided.

Kind of makes a man feel like he's back in the States. Lisa always loved coming home to Prescott. Especially in the spring! I should stop in on the Nashes . . . maybe they've . . .

He had left Arizona Territory to help him forget the past, but it was the past that called him back. Two years had taught him only that he would never outlive or outrun what happened on that Christmas day. He didn't like thinking about it . . . but it was always there, like priceless nuggets lying on the surface of his memory.

He thought about trying to find the Barton home. Mail would be waiting for him. But the sun had already set behind the western hills.

If I were out on the prairie someplace, I wouldn't hesitate to barge in and have supper with total strangers. But in town . . . in a town like this it probably wouldn't be proper. And I've got a feeling Miss Harriet does things proper.

Instead Brannon rode down Second Street and pulled up at the Hassayampa Hotel. Tying El Viento to the rail, he unfastened his bedroll and clomped across the wooden sidewalk to the hotel's entrance.

His clothes were caked thick with road dust.

His spurs sang wildly as he walked.

His Winchester swung from his right hand.

His bedroll was tucked under his left arm.

His crusty black hat was pushed back just a tad.

"Stuart, welcome back to the Hassayampa!"

Brannon turned to a well-dressed man in a gray frocked coat and wire-framed eyeglasses.

"Roberts? You still here? I figured you'd be rich and moved to San Francisco by now!"

"Rich? On hotel manager's wages? You're the one who wandered up to the San Juans and struck gold . . . we heard about your mine!" Roberts chided.

"Yeah, well, as you can see I spent it all on clothes!"

"You know, Stuart," Byron Roberts continued, "the only easy money I ever made in this town was the night I bet you could whip all four of the Boswells."

"What did you do with all that money?"

"Saved it until this year. Then I got married. Didn't you hear?"

"Married!" Brannon stepped back and surveyed the large Scottish innkeeper. "Congratulations! Who's the bride?"

Roberts smiled and shook his head. "You wouldn't know her . . . she just moved to town last fall. An eastern girl. And smart. Wait until you meet her, Stuart. She thinks we ought to start a college out here. Can you imagine that? A college?"

"Not . . . Harriet . . ."

"Harriet? You mean Gwen Barton's sister? My word, now there's a woman who puts fear into every prospector and cowhand's heart. They treat her like she was Athene herself. Of course she keeps mainly to herself. But when she walks down the sidewalk, half the saloon empties out into the street. No woman's caught the town's fancy like that since . . ." Roberts stopped and glanced down.

"It's OK. Go ahead and say it."

"Well . . . since your Lisa was here. You know, Stuart, you aren't the only one who misses her. Maybe it's good that Miss Harriet moved to town. Helps folks go on."

"Well, I'm on my way back to the ranch. I don't aim to leave Arizona again. Now who is the lucky Mrs. Roberts?"

"Mary Katherine Warner from Omaha, Nebraska. She's needing to rest this evening or I'd be introducing you. A baby, you know. Doc says it should be here by December."

"Congratulations again, Byron. That's the kind of news that makes my day!"

"We got your room ready for you."

"My room? I haven't been here in two years!"

"I know, but it's been buzzing around town for a couple of hours that you were headed to Prescott, so I knew you'd want the room on the corner, overlooking the sidewalk. They say you took a knife and sliced your way through two dozen Apaches to rescue those soldier boys."

"Well, thanks, Byron. It's nice to get back to where a few folks know your name and no one ever exaggerates the truth!"

"I can tell you one thing, Stuart. Everyone in Prescott knows your name. Your ranch might be miles away, but you're a local boy to most folks here. So when those stories started filtering into the newspaper—"

"What stories?"

"You know . . . about the shootout in that meadow . . . standing up to that railroad man . . . what's his name?"

"Cheney?"

"Yeah, him. And Trevor, and sheriffing at Tres Casas. We had a note last week that you and a schoolteacher cleaned up some two-bit grubstake town."

"That was in print?"

Roberts nodded. "Yep. You been out living our lives for us, Stuart. Ever' shopkeeper, sod turner, soldier, and hard-rock miner came out to this country to live adventures like yours. We don't have the skill or the courage. But you're our man. The day will come when this desert will be a state, and it will be as tame as an Ohio farm. Then a few of us old-timers will sit out there on the porch and spin yarns about the early days . . . days when men like Stuart Brannon tamed the West, yes, sir!"

"Roberts, I had no idea you were such a philosopher. That edu-

cated wife of yours must have really rubbed off on you." Brannon
headed for the stairs to the second floor. "Byron, thanks for the
room. I'll only need it a few days."

"I'd offer to buy you supper, but the rumor is you've got some
big doin's planned at the Lucky Dollar."

"That's what I hear." Brannon climbed the stairs to his room.

A basin of water, a change of shirts, and a comb through his
hair, and Brannon was ready. It was still a little early, so he pulled
off his boots and sprawled across the top of the bed.

He never cared much for staying in hotel rooms. But the mattress at the Hassayampa Hotel was softer than spring grass on the
south slope.

Ten minutes and I'll feel a whole lot better.

"Mr. Brannon!"

The room was dark.

"Mr. Brannon!"

Someone was beating on the door.

"Stuart?"

He staggered across the room, grabbed up his Winchester, and
slung open the door. Byron Roberts and Sergeant Cloverdale
stood outside.

"You feel like havin' that supper now?" Cloverdale asked.

"What time is it?"

"A little past 9:30." The sergeant apologized, "I'm sorry. If
you'd rather wait, the boys will—"

"No . . . nope, I'm plenty hungry. The old Hassayampa's got
the best mattress between Chicago and San Francisco. Guess my
bones were more tired than I knew. Let me grab my boots!"

Brannon tucked his trousers into his stove-top boots, splashed
a little dirty water on his face, jammed his hat on his head, and
headed out of the room.

"Byron, can you see that someone takes El Viento over to the
livery? I'd appreciate it."

"Two Fingers, I suppose," Roberts replied.

"Yeah . . . how is that old man, anyway?"

"Sober . . . most of the time."

Brannon and the sergeant walked the three blocks to the Lucky Dollar.

"Looks like payday at the mines," Brannon offered. "Street's crowded. It's not Saturday night, is it?"

"No, sir."

Glancing at the soldiers loitering on the front steps, Brannon turned to the sergeant. "Who's minding the store at the barracks?"

"To tell you the truth, most of the men wanted to come to town tonight. I think it's mainly the officers that are left out there."

"Well, the Lucky Dollar must have a new cook or some dancing girls to draw a crowd like this."

"Mr. Brannon." One of the uniformed men approached him. "My name's Jenner, sir. Eli Taylor was my closest friend."

"Taylor? Out on the trail? Sure am sorry about it, Jenner. I hoped we could make it to the doctor."

"Well, sir, when me and him signed on, we knew we'd be fightin' hostiles. Thanks to you, he could die in the saddle, singing a song after a brave fight. No torture, no mutilations, no shame. Mr. Brannon, that means a whole lot to me."

"Will you be burying him tomorrow?"

"Yes, sir, we will."

"Jenner, you find the best baritone in the barracks and have him sing 'Annie Laurie' at the grave."

"Yes, sir."

Several more men came up to shake hands with Brannon, including some in civilian clothes.

"Mr. Brannon!"

"Barton? Nelson Barton, good to see you again."

"Welcome back to Prescott, Mr. Brannon. Harriet will be extremely jealous that I saw you before she did."

"Please tell her that she was certainly the first one I thought about visiting, but I just didn't think it proper to go calling at this hour without a formal invite."

Barton smiled and tipped his hat. "I will certainly tell her that. I say sincerely, you have an open invitation to our home."

"Might I impose then for supper tomorrow? I would like to come calling."

"We would be insulted if you didn't. She's holding several letters and telegrams that came for you. Come early. I'd like to discuss this land grant business . . . things have been quite confusing lately."

"I look forward to it."

"Shall I tell the ladies you'll arrive at 5:00 P.M.?"

"My pleasure, but give me a little slack on the time. Last minute delays have a way of ambushing me."

"I'll see you tomorrow. It looks like you're having quite a party at the Lucky Dollar."

"Oh no," Brannon explained, "I think this is payday or something—right, Sergeant?"

"Actually . . . it's for you, Mr. Brannon."

Inside the Lucky Dollar, over fifty men crammed the tables and the bar. A big U.S. flag draped the back wall. As Brannon and Cloverdale worked their way through the crowd, the uniformed soldiers stood and saluted.

"I think this is getting a little a . . . blown out of proportion," he whispered to the sergeant.

"These men need an excuse to relax. There haven't been many success stories lately. You just rode in at the right time," Cloverdale replied under his breath.

A place of honor was waiting for Brannon. It wouldn't have been his choice. But he sat down and visited with several men.

My back to the door . . . crowded room . . . rifle on the floor. Maybe in Prescott. But never in Tres Casas, or Tombstone, or Silver City.

The food began rolling out the second he sat down. Boiled potatoes by the bowl, fresh corn, beans and salsa, grits, a whole platter of sizzling steaks, stewed tomatoes, pickled eggs, baskets of biscuits, slabs of fresh butter, cherry preserves, pitchers of milk, and coffee, coffee, and more coffee. Finally, after almost an hour, an apple pie and a huge peach cobbler, still warm, arrived at the table.

During the meal Brannon figured every man in the room had

spent time at his table, some helping him eat, most just wanting to talk.

Lord, it feels good, real good, not to have to shoot my way in and out of a town. Thanks for the homecoming!

He was talking with a short, blond corporal from El Paso who knew his sister, when a faint click in the noisy room sent chills down his back. It was the cocked hammer of a Colt, not more than six inches behind his head.

"You ain't no hero to me, Stuart Brannon!" a man sneered. "You move those hands below the table and you're dead."

Brannon tried to glance behind him, but he met the barrel of a .45. Suddenly, others in the room saw what had happened, and dozens of guns were pointed at the man.

"Drop the gun, Mister!" Cloverdale shouted.

"I ain't . . . you boys open up and bullets will go flying everywhere. And this bullet is going through Brannon's head."

"You can't make it out of here alive," someone shouted.

"Neither can Stuart Brannon. Which of you wants to be the one that caused his death? Stand up! We're going for a walk. Keep those hands up."

Brannon stood and faced the man with the gun.

The man's eyes were bloodshot, and he had a nervous twitch in his left eye. The Colt was old, well worn in from use.

"I don't know you," he told the man.

"Nope. But you shot down my brother in Colorado."

"Where did I do that?"

"On the Denver road, north of Conchita."

"He was robbing a stage and trying to kill me—"

"He was my only brother. 'An eye for an eye,' the Good Book states, and I aim to collect!"

"A U.S. Marshal was murdered by your brother and the others. Now that settles the score."

"Back out of this room, Brannon!"

"No . . . I think I'll stay right here."

"I'll shoot ya!"

"So what?"

"You'll die, that's what!"

"And then what?"

"What do you mean?"

"When I'm dead, lying on the floor, what happens then?"

"I'd say about a hundred bullets will pass through various parts of his body." Cloverdale never took his gun off the man.

"Mister, why don't you holster that pistol and walk back out that door?" Brannon insisted. "Don't let your whiskey and the dark make you do something you wouldn't try in daylight."

"It ain't right. You don't deserve to live! Besides, if I back out now, they'll shoot me down!" he hollered.

"Nobody's going to get shot." Brannon was speaking in a soft, slow whisper. "Go get yourself some black coffee and then ride out of town. Your mama doesn't want to lose two boys . . ."

The young man froze, then started to shoot, but by then it was too late. Brannon's raised right hand yanked the man's hat down over his eyes. At the same moment with his left hand Brannon grabbed the gun hand and shoved it straight up. A hurried shot exploded through the ceiling. Then a left jab in the chin followed by a right cross brought the man to his knees. He toppled on his face. Several strong arms pinned him there.

"Take his gun, boys, and toss him out of here. Whiskey brave doesn't win many battles."

Without another word, the man was bodily carried out into the street.

"He's not very happy," Cloverdale warned.

"He'll wake up smarter," Brannon offered. "Sorry to dampen this party. But to tell you the truth, I'm worn out. How about calling it a day? I sure do want to thank you all for the meal. I spent six months in the mountains of Colorado dreaming about a supper like this."

"Do you need an escort?" Cloverdale offered.

"Gentlemen, save your escort for tomorrow's funeral. I'll be fine. It's just that—"

A scream from the second story of the Lucky Dollar silenced everyone in the room. A young lady in a long green dress ran down the stairs. "Julie's been shot! She's bleeding bad! A bullet came through the floor! Get a doctor! Hurry!"

An ice cold chill rolled up Brannon's back and into his neck.

"No . . . no . . . no . . . !" He ran to the stairs and leaped three at a time to make it to the top before the others. The door swung open to the little dark room that sported only a worn-out settee, a wall shelf, and a bed. Lying on the floor in a faded gold satin dress, Brannon discovered a young lady bleeding profusely from the side.

He ripped a sheet off the bed and folded it, pressing it against the wound. Then he propped up her head on a pillow and stared into her eyes.

"Miss, we've got a doctor coming . . . we'll get you fixed up real soon."

"Why?" she cried. "Why would anyone want to shoot me? I didn't do nothin'!"

"Don't try to talk, Miss. It was . . . an accident. Just a scuffle downstairs and a stray bullet. No one was gunning for you."

"Did you shoot me?"

Brannon took a deep breath and pushed his hat back. By now several others crowded in the door. Her long black curls matted her face. Her dark eyes peered out in terror.

"No, Miss . . . I didn't shoot."

"Is she dead?" someone from the hall shouted.

"Get the doc. Quick!" Brannon hollered back.

"I can't move my legs!" she sobbed.

"Miss . . . Julie, isn't it?"

She nodded. "Julie Cancino."

"Miss Cancino, it might be that the bullet's lodged in there keeping you from moving. The doc may have to dig it out."

"I don't have any money to pay a doctor!" she moaned.

"That's the least of your worries. I'll take care of the cost of things."

"Why?" She sucked air, trying to get another breath into her lungs. The tears rolled across her smooth, clean cheeks.

"'Cause I was the one he was shooting at."

"Who are you, Mister?" she gasped.

"Stuart Brannon."

"Yeah," she whispered, "and I'm the Queen of Sheba. Are you

really Brannon?" She closed her eyes, and Brannon could see she
was a very attractive woman.

The next several hours were a confusion of emotions and
actions. The doctor came and immediately ordered the girl
brought to his office. Brannon carried her down the stairs, along
the wooden sidewalk, across the darkened street, and into the doctor's office. A trail of blood marked his course. His shirt, trousers,
arms, and hands were splattered red.

Another doctor was quickly summoned. With help from the
other girl from the Lucky Dollar, they probed for the bullet.
Brannon pushed the spectators out of the office and waited outside on the sidewalk for the report.

Most of the soldiers headed back out to the barracks.

One by one the townspeople slipped back home through the
shadows.

"It's taking them a long time," Sergeant Cloverdale remarked.

"It was bad," Brannon mumbled, "real bad."

"Nothing you could have done about it. Just one of those acci-
dents."

"I could have stayed out of Prescott. She'd never have gotten
shot."

"That ain't your fault."

"Cloverdale, I don't understand. I'll never understand it. Five
days ago I faced down four bushwhackers and rode off without
a scratch. Then I stumbled into a dozen Apaches on the prod and
rode off unscathed. Now this girl is just sitting in her room, and
she gets shot. It's crazy . . . it's just not right!"

"Brannon, you did all you could. When she hired on at the
Lucky Dollar, she knew the kind of place it was. It's not like she's
from the other side of town . . . I mean, she's just a—"

The sergeant was almost lifted off the bench by Brannon's
bloody right hand around his neck.

"I don't care who she is or isn't. She deserves better than this!"
he snapped. Then he released his grip. "Sergeant . . . I'm sorry . . .
I'm just mightily upset by all of this."

"Brannon, that's about the first normal human reaction I've

seen out of you. Don't apologize for hurtin'. I'm going on out to the barracks. You know if you need anything, just . . ."

"Thanks. I know you mean it. Tell the boys I really appreciated the dinner. Sometime, about fall, you're all invited down to the ranch for a little cookout at my place."

"I'll tell 'em." The sergeant stood to leave. "I hear the sheriff's searching town to arrest that bushwhacker."

"He's probably ten miles down the road already."

"Yeah . . . I suppose. Well, good night, Brannon."

Brannon sat alone for a long time.

Lord, this thing about providence is mighty hard to understand. I talked about it so easy . . . but please don't let her die. Give her a chance to do something more in life . . .

"Mr. Brannon?"

He jumped to his feet as one of the doctors came out of the office.

"Yes, sir," he blurted out, "how is she?"

"Mr. Brannon, I'm Dr. Levine. Miss Cancino is extremely serious, as you could see. We don't know if she'll pull through the night. We got the bullet out, but there was damage to the spine."

"Spine? Can she use her legs?"

"Time will tell. The next twenty-four hours are critical. There's a threat of pneumonia, infection, and even a heart stoppage. The shock on her body has been critical."

"What can I do?"

"Just wait . . . and pray. Dr. Matthewson will stay with her the first shift; then I'll come back and relieve him."

"Do you mind if I wait out here?"

"Help yourself. I'll see you later."

"Look, Doc, thanks. I mentioned to the other doctor that I'd cover the costs. If you need some funds up front, I could—"

"We'll settle up later. I can assure you, Mr. Brannon, she'll receive the best care that we know how to give."

Brannon tipped his hat. "I appreciate it."

After about an hour, one of the men from the Lucky Dollar stopped by and brought Brannon his jacket and his Winchester from the cafe.

Far into the night Brannon spied someone carrying a lantern coming closer—a slow, deliberate advance through the dark.

A woman? At this hour?

With dark hair tied behind her head and wearing an off-white dress, she floated down the street like a swan on a pond.

"Miss Harriet?" Brannon stood to his feet and yanked off his hat. "What in the world are you doing—"

"I couldn't sleep. I heard all about what happened at the Lucky Dollar. How is she?"

"Still out. They won't know much until tomorrow or the next day. It's good to see you, Miss Reed. I've thought of you often."

"Well . . . to tell you the truth, Mr. Brannon, I've been wondering for three months what it would be like to see you again."

"And this isn't exactly the way you had it figured?"

"Hardly." She held the lamp high and glanced at Brannon. "You're a mess! Are you injured?"

"No, I don't get hurt . . . it seems I just cause pain to others."

"May I sit down?"

"Certainly." He motioned and they sat on the bench. "Miss Harriet, are you sure you want to be out here this time of the night . . . or morning? I'll walk you back home. I mean, some folks would talk about—"

"Mr. Brannon, I'm quite capable of looking after my own reputation without your help or the community's."

"Yes, ma'am, I'm sure you are."

"I brought your letters. I thought you might like to read them."

Brannon stood and hung the lantern on a bent nail in the beam above their heads.

"This one's from Velvet Shepherd in Tres Casas. I believe I heard that she married the mayor."

"Yep. He's a fine doctor, too." Brannon quickly scanned Vel's letter. "This is good, this is good," he muttered. "Rose is teaching school there. She got the job."

"Rose?"

"Rose Creek from up at Paradise Meadow. She was—"

"Then the stories about you are true!"

"What stories?"

"That you and a schoolteacher stood up against the whole town."

"Well, that's close."

"And here's one from San Francisco. Tell me, Mr. Brannon, why do people keep sending your mail to me?"

"Because I don't know many folks who sit still long enough to have an address. And, well . . . because I guess I wanted an excuse to stop by for a visit."

"Well, in that case," she said with a nod, "please continue to have your mail sent here. Now who's that one from?"

"Fletcher! You met Edwin, didn't you?"

"Just briefly. English, isn't he?"

"Quite!" Brannon laughed. "Let's see . . . he settled matters at the consulate, picked up his papers and all . . . and will meet me at the ranch by the first week in June." Then Brannon held the letter closer to the light. "What? I don't believe it. Deedra and Darrlyn?"

"Who?"

"The Lazzard twins!"

"Oh? How old are they?"

"Eh . . . maybe twenty or so. I don't know. From Boston? Listen to this:

> Well, incredible as it seems, they now claim they are not helpless pilgrims but proper Bostonians who traveled across the country on a lark. Both seem quite well educated and Dristina (Deedra) is engaged to a British attaché here in the city. Darlena (Darrlyn) is the talk of the town, seen lately with none other than Count DuVaul. They send you greetings. The dinner offer is still valid.

> My greetings to the charming Miss Reed.

"That's the wildest story I've ever heard of! You should have met these girls. They—"

"At twenty they were ladies, not girls," she corrected. "Here's one more letter. From the Indian Territory."

"Elizabeth?" Brannon tore open the letter to find a sealed envelope inside.

"It's my letter! Returned! She didn't get my letter!"

"What does it say on the outside?"

"'Cannot locate addressee.' Can't locate her? What do they mean? She just sent me a letter. Of course she's there!"

"The other letter was mailed months ago. Perhaps the situation has changed."

"But she's somewhere! I mean, the government shipped her back there; they surely keep track of her!"

"Now, this Elizabeth is Indian, correct?"

"Yeah . . . Nez Perce."

"Mr. Brannon, have you ever noticed how your life seems to revolve around women?"

"What?"

"Velvet, Rose, Deedra, Darrlyn, Elizabeth . . . and now you're sitting here because of some girl named July."

"Julie. Yeah, and you didn't mention Harriet Reed."

"Nor Lisa."

"How do you know about my Lisa?"

"From Mr. and Mrs. Nash."

"You know Lisa's parents?"

"Yes, we often run into each other at church."

"Then you know about her death?"

"Not really. That seems to be a topic they would rather not discuss."

"Well, would you like for me to tell you about Lisa . . . and the others?"

"Only if you want to."

FOUR

Can you imagine doing something like that back home? All night long, until sunlight began to reflect from the tips of the tallest pines. It was cold, and my scanty lavender shawl hardly warmed my shoulders, but I couldn't leave.

I must say I didn't want to leave.

And it wasn't just a schoolgirl's infatuation. I am (and so are you!) much too old for that. There is something of almost epic proportions about the West. Everything is big, vast, towering. The mountains, the plains, the rivers, the valleys . . . my, we have cacti that stand twenty feet or more. Most people seem so dwarfed—lives so small—you get a feeling that you're viewing all of life, even your own, from a distance.

But then, a few people come along, and they aren't small. They ride or walk or run through this country as if given a special sense to experience all of its grandeur. Mr. Brannon, I should say Stuart (he asked me to please call him Stuart!), is such a man. Here's this man—about thirty, brown hair (it could use a trim), blue-gray eyes, strong shoulders, and rugged handsome face—sitting on a bench in front of a doctor's office. He's covered from boot to hat with the blood of a wounded cafe girl, and he's telling me the story of his life.

I kept looking around half expecting to see a historian with note pad and pen jotting down scenes for his next book. Out here there isn't always an opportunity to read history because one is too busy making it.

Yes, he is quite the man I expected. Only don't believe all those newspaper accounts of shootings. I'll let you know what is really happening. I do believe we have established a relationship that will grow. You simply must come out and meet him! I can tell he's a God-fearing man, just by his casual references. He will be coming over to the house for supper tonight, and then he asked if he could escort me to church on Sunday.

Well, he walked me home around 6:00 A.M.

No, we didn't touch (girl, I know what you are thinking!).

I will try to write to you on Monday—if I can find the time.

Give my best to Rachel.

Affectionately yours,
Miss Harriet Reed

It was almost noon when Brannon woke up and rolled out of bed at the Hassayampa Hotel. He pulled back the curtains and allowed the bright Arizona sun to ease him awake. The streets of Prescott hummed with activity. Folks buying supplies. Cowboys loitering on street corners. Miners and prospectors huddled on the steps of their favorite saloon. Opening the door of his room just a tad, he found a stack of neatly folded clothes waiting for him.

Once dressed, he tied a new bandanna around his neck, combed his hair, and slipped on his hat. Strapping on his hand-gun, he glanced over at the rifle propped up against the corner. He started out the door, then turned back, picked up the Winchester, and headed down to the lobby.

"Mornin', Stuart. Kind of a rough night?" Byron Roberts greeted him.

"I suppose you heard all about it?"

"Yep. Plus I read it in the paper this morning."

"In the paper already?"

"I guess they worked all night over there. Both the Apache raid and the shooting at the Lucky Dollar."

"Say, these clothes cleaned up real fine. What did you do to get out those stains?"

"I used an ancient family method."

"What's that?"

"I took them to a Chinese laundry. Look, I stopped by the doc's."

"How's Julie?"

"She's burning up. Doc fears gangrene . . . but she wants to see you real bad."

"I was planning to stop by on my way to the Bartons. Say, did the sheriff catch that old boy who fired the gun?"

"Rumor is that he just lit out on his pony in a run heading south."

"Just as well, I suppose. Look, I'll be staying on until Sunday at least. Promised Harriet I'd go to church with them."

"If you keep being seen around town with Miss Harriet, all sorts of rumors will fly," Roberts said laughing.

"Well, if anyone starts casting disparaging remarks about her, they'll have to answer directly to me."

"Brannon, there's not a sober man in this town that would think of getting you riled. We're just all hoping Miss Harriet will settle you down."

Brannon laughed and ambled out into the street. He slowed down behind a man, woman, and several small children who dawdled along behind. The smallest stood staring in a window, smiling at his own reflection. Brannon waited for them to move on.

"Lawrence, hurry along now!" the mother called.

The youngster whipped around towards Brannon and shouted, "Daddy . . ." Then he realized he was addressing the wrong man. Flushed a deep red, he ran on up to his parents.

"Say, aren't you Stuart Brannon?" the husband called.

"Yes, sir, I am. Have we met?"

"Oh, no. I, eh . . . have a little place south of town. We just heard about you, that's all. I'm William Torvell, and this is my wife Emmy Mae, and Lorenda, Lucinda, Lalanda, and Lawrence."

Brannon shook hands with each one. All three girls curtsied nicely, but Lawrence hid behind his mother's skirt.

"How old is Lawrence, ma'am? About two, two and a half?"

"Yes." She smiled. "He was born on the day after Christmas, two and a half years ago."

"Well." Brannon took a deep breath. "The Lord bless you, son. I was mighty proud even for a minute to be reckoned as your father."

He tipped his hat to the woman and scooted on past. As he did, he heard one of the girls say, "Is that the real Stuart Brannon, Daddy?"

Sweetheart, the real Stuart Brannon has to fight like a cougar to hold back the tears every time he sees a little two-year-old boy. Somehow they never put that part in the newspaper.

He waited for a couple of wagons to pass on the road. Then he crossed the street and hiked up the sidewalk to the doctor's office.

It was the older physician, Dr. Levine, who greeted him.

"Good afternoon, Mr. Brannon."

"Mornin' . . . I mean, afternoon. Doc, how's the patient?"

He flung his hands in the air and shrugged. "What can I say? She's conscious . . . the bullet's been removed . . . the external bleeding has stopped . . ."

"But?"

"I would not say her chances are real positive. The human body, as a man like yourself knows, is not meant to survive the impact of gunfire."

"Look, Doc, isn't there anything else you can do? I'm not criticizing, mind you, but if there's some medicine or procedure, I'm prepared to wire San Francisco and have them send the—"

"Mr. Brannon, I will accept the sincerity of your concern, but you will have to accept the accuracy of mine. There is nothing doctors at Harvard, or anywhere else could do for her. If that body can heal itself, it will . . . if it cannot, it will give up. There is nothing we can do but wait. I know that is frustrating. I have spent my career being frustrated."

"You don't mind if I pray for her, do you, Doc?"

"Divine intervention is always welcome. But please step in

there and talk to her. You seem to be the only one she is interested in seeing."

Brannon went through the door into a small room. Julie Cancino lay still in a bed encased in white sheets and covered with a heavy quilt. Her eyes were closed, and her head faced the door.

She'd be the first one every cowboy would pick at the dance! She's beautiful!

Everything was so quiet that Brannon heard his spurs jingle even as he stepped lightly across the wooden floor.

Lord, I don't have any pious words left in me. I want this girl healed. I want her strong enough to laugh and sing and run down the road. And I don't want it just to make me feel better. Give her another chance, please. Give her one of my chances if You can—

"You just gonna stand there?" a weak voice interrupted his prayer.

"No, ma'am, I didn't want to wake you."

"What were you doing? Staring at me? I look a fright. One of the girls is coming over to comb my hair later on."

"No, ma'am, I wasn't staring . . . I was praying."

"Prayin'? But I ain't dead . . . yet."

"I kind of figure prayers do some good before we die."

"You really are Brannon, aren't you?"

"Yes, ma'am."

"Well, I'll be . . . you know what Sylvia says?"

"Sylvia?"

"Over at the Lucky Dollar. She said, 'Julie, you'll be in the history books. Shot down by a bullet meant for Stuart Brannon!'"

"I'm counting on you pullin' through all this and creating your own history."

"Did the doctor tell you how bad it is? It's bad; I know it's bad."

"Yep. He told me."

"You know, I always figured I could take a lot of pain. But not this much! The lower part of my body won't move. It just torments me somethin' fierce!"

"I've heard of cases where the movement returns after a few days."

"Yeah, and I've seen some that was dead within two days. Mr. Stuart Brannon, do you know what I was doing when I got shot?"

"No, ma'am."

"I was up in my room getting ready to put on my blue party dress because me and Sylvia had a bet on which one of us could be the first to get a kiss from Mr. Stuart Brannon."

"You what?"

"Yep. We heard you were coming to the Lucky Dollar, so we made this bet. And not on the cheek neither. It had to be a kiss on the lips."

Brannon just stood there and stared at her frightened brown eyes.

"Anyway," she murmured, "I hear the man who shot me escaped."

"That's what I understand."

"You'll hunt him down, won't you, Mr. Brannon?"

"Well, I'm not sure the sheriff needs my help."

"Mr. Brannon . . ."

"Call me Stuart."

"I'm Julie." She looked for a moment like she was trying to smile. "Are you afraid of dying, Mr. . . . I mean, Stuart?"

"Julie, some days I'm afraid of livin' and some days afraid of dyin', and some days I'm afraid of both."

"Well, if I'm going to die, I'd like it to be soon. I'm tired, real tired."

"Julie, I expect to see you up and dancing in a few weeks."

"Would you dance with me?"

"You are looking at the world's worst dancer. I'm afraid I would embarrass you."

"Would you dance with me . . . Stuart?"

"Miss Julie . . . I'll dance with you. Someday you'll be the only woman in this town who danced with Stuart Brannon. Believe me, it's not much of an honor."

"I'll look forward to it."

"I got things arranged with the doctors to cover your expenses, so if you need anything—anything at all—you tell them. I've got to go have some supper, but I'll be checking up on you every day until I leave."

"You're going out of town?"

"In a few days. I've got a ranch to go visit."

"How will I get that dance?"

"You let me know; I'll be here. It's a guarantee."

"What about Miss Reed?"

"Miss Reed?"

"Some folks say Miss Reed has her eyes on you."

"She'll just have to wait in line," Brannon chided.

For a moment the pain eased in her eyes. "Why, I'm so sorry, Miss Reed," she mocked, "Stuart and I have this dance. You'll have to wait over there with the old maids."

I'll bet she can really dance.

He leaned over and brushed her hair back behind her ear, and leaving his hand there, bent low and gently kissed her on the lips.

"You win the bet, Miss Julie."

"I sure did, didn't I!" she said. "Thanks. You didn't have to do that."

"That's where you're wrong," he murmured. "It's the one thing I did have to do! Now I'll come see you again tomorrow."

"I'll be counting on it."

Brannon placed his black hat back on his head and quietly closed the door behind him. He picked up his Winchester that lay in the corner of the office and nodded at the doctor who was busy with another patient.

There was absolutely nothing about the busy Prescott street that hinted at such a life-and-death struggle nearby.

Death happens.

Every day.

But only to other people.

At least, that's what we all hope.

He walked the rest of the way to the Barton home without speaking to anyone.

Brannon felt rough, awkward, and out of place in the Barton dining room. Silver forks. China plates. Crystal glasses. He kept a close eye on Gwendolyn Barton, making sure he used the right utensil at the right time.

The food, on the other hand, was delicious and the conversation, warm and interesting.

"I apologize, Mrs. Barton, for dressing so casually. I've spent most of my life eating on the ground or in some crowded cafe."

"I can assure you, Mr. Brannon, no apologies are needed. One thing I enjoy about the West is the freedom for everyone to be himself. This . . . this is the stuffy, formal Bartons. I suppose we will always be. But don't let that change you."

"And if you can't stomach any of this cuisine," Nelson Barton added, "please just leave it."

"The food is excellent."

"Well, Harriet is our meal planner, so you'll have to give her the credit."

As he continued to eat, he glanced over at Harriet Reed. Her light yellow dress stood in contrast to Gwendolyn Barton's dark blue. The multicolored scarf was not draped like a shawl, as was the fashion, but tied more like a bandanna.

Almost perfect.

A little tilt to the scarf.

One strand of hair, a little reckless, not quite pulled back.

Her ring slipped on the smallest finger. The sleeves ever so slightly rolled up.

Could there be a casual streak in Miss Reed after all?

When he wasn't looking at her, she was quietly examining him.
This is silly. Girlish. I can't believe I did this. A bandanna? Mussed hair? Turned-up sleeves? And that gaudy ring? Harriet, if you giggle . . . if you giggle just once, I promise I will throw you off the highest cliff in Arizona! You are not now nor will ever be ranch-raised.

On the other hand, I do believe Mr. Stuart Brannon would look quite handsome with a long coat and—

"I say, Stuart, what are your plans for the coming week?" Nelson Barton asked.

"Well, I need to send a few letters back to the Indian Territory. Elizabeth is there someplace, and I've got to track her down. Then I'll buy a pair of driving horses and a few supplies for the ranch. I feel obligated to hang around and see how Miss Cancino is progressing."

"Stuart says he will be leaving fairly soon. He must return to his cherished Ithaca," Harriet broke in.

"I've only been gone two years, not twenty . . . so I don't feel much like Odysseus."

"And you're not the type to succumb to Calypso's imprisonment?"

"When I see you weaving cloth on a golden spool, I know I'll be in trouble."

"You have read well, Mr. Brannon," Mrs. Barton approved.

"It was a long time ago, ma'am. But if I remember the story, Telemachus and his beautiful mother Penelope were waiting for him at home. All I've got are an adobe ranch house and title to the hillside."

"Oh, yes. I'm terribly sorry. It was a thoughtless analogy, and I had no business making the comparison. Forgive me," Harriet said blushing.

"No cause for concern," Brannon reassured her. "Except for those last hours, all my memories of Lisa are good. It's not a pain to stir up those thoughts."

"Speaking of your ranch . . ." Mr. Barton slid his chair back. "Say, would you like to join me on the front porch? It's too nice a day to lounge inside."

The men took their places in two white Chinese wicker chairs on the porch.

"Stuart . . . a cigar?" Barton offered.

Brannon leaned his head back on the chair and closed his eyes. "No thanks, Nelson . . . just relaxin' here in this comfortable chair is about all the pleasure I can soak in at once."

"As I began inside," Barton continued, "I retrieved your ranch papers from our vault as you requested. We would be happy to

keep them here as long as you want. But I don't blame you for taking them with you. Land titles have been quite bizarre for the past
several months."

"What do you mean?"

"Well, we seem to have an abundance of people in Arizona who
need a quick dollar. There are schemes all over the Territory for
selling real estate that doesn't belong to them. Not to mention the
problem of Spanish land grants."

"Yeah, I heard about that—selling phony papers and all."

"I don't know how long this land grant business will be tying
things up. Every resident of Spanish heritage seems to have a grant
and is willing to sell his share for $200. The stories are incredible.
Just yesterday, a man named Willing, Dr. Willing, a patent
medicine salesman from St Louis, or somewhere . . . anyway he
barges into my office and demands we give our approval to his
so-called land grant before he takes it to the Surveyor-General.

"Well, I'm not in the habit of giving my opinion of any land
grant documents before they are filed, but in this case I made an
exception. Listen to this—he claimed to have purchased from a
Mexican man named Miquel Peralta a grant for over 18,000
square miles!"

"That sounds like half the state! What would that be—ten,
maybe twelve million acres?"

"Precisely. I tried to hint that it was ludicrous. They tell me
they're about to make purposely filing false claims a crime. That
should slow some of them down."

"Hopefully, more folks won't get suckered in."

"Yet, with the influx of gullible people, I would imagine you'll
be able to buy a 'genuine' land grant on any corner."

"Well, I suppose it makes your job more interesting."

"It's not boring. Most folks get pretty excited when the matter turns to land ownership. I hear you're planning to return to
ranching."

"Well, that's about all I know. I guess I'll keep at it until I go
broke again. Then I'll head off to the gold fields and raise me
another stake."

"What if you succeed in ranching?"

Brannon turned to Barton and laughed. "Now that, Nelson, is a possibility that I've never considered."

"May we join you?" Miss Reed broke in.

"Certainly." Brannon and Barton stood as the women sat together on a porch swing.

"Men's talk, I presume?"

"Yes, Brannon and I were debating whether the dancing girls in Virginia City are as skillful as those in Abilene."

"As you can see, Nelson has a very wicked sense of humor!" Miss Reed scolded.

"But an effective way of changing the subject." Brannon smiled.

For almost three hours the four of them talked of politics, religion, Arizona weather, the plight of world affairs, classic literature, and the need for a clear national policy for handling Indian affairs.

By the time Brannon walked back to the Hassayampa Hotel, he realized it was the first relaxing, thoughtfully stimulating evening he'd spent in three years.

He shoved the bed to the far side of the room, leaned the Winchester against the nightstand, draped the holster over the bedstead, blew out the light, and crawled under the covers.

He went to sleep without worrying about ambushes, flying bullets, or attacking Indians. He was not pushing cattle down the trail, breaking horses, or feeding sick calves. Rather he was drafting a telegram in his mind to the Secretary of War, soliciting the reinstatement of General Crook to lead the troops in Arizona.

Morning sun was on the street by the time he swung out of bed. The deep sleep fell away quickly and he felt refreshed. No aches and pains from sleeping on the ground. No tired bones from spending the previous day in the saddle. No vigilantes to subdue, no outlaws to apprehend, no drunks to arrest. As he stared out on the quiet street, for the first time in his life Brannon briefly considered running for political office. It would be the last time he had such a thought.

For four days he repeated the same routine.

Mornings with Miss Julie.

Afternoons buying supplies.
Evenings with the Bartons.
Only Sunday was different.

Having borrowed a rather ill-fitting long coat and tie from
Nelson Barton, Brannon slipped into the fourth pew back, next
to Harriet Reed. In some ways the church looked the same as on
the day he and Lisa were married in it. The tall, narrow side windows cast beams of light that seemed to draw his attention to the
pulpit. The wooden floor was polished. The brass candlesticks
gleamed. The rich oak wood was as solid as the faith of the pio-
neers who had built the church.

The singing was robust. The prayers fervent. The preaching
pointed.

Too pointed.

"Violent men create a violent society . . . godly men create a
godly society."

He shook the preacher's hand, but thought it best not to linger.
Recognizing an older face in the crowd, he scooted over to visit.

"Mr. Nash! I wanted to say hello."

"Stuart! Why, I knew you were in town, of course, but was
afraid our trails wouldn't cross."

"How have you been?"

"Well, you know how my back is. Some days I could wrestle a
bear, and other times I can't stand up. I've been keeping up with
you through the papers. Quite a little jaunt up in Colorado, I
hear."

"Yes, sir, but it's good to be home. How is Mrs. Nash? I didn't
see her with you. Perhaps I could stop by later and—"

"Stuart, I'll be straight up with you because I know that's the
way you want it. Emily . . . Mrs. Nash has had a relapse this week.
She's deeply sad. Can't control her crying. Won't eat. Can't sleep."

"I thought maybe by this time she . . ."

"You know, Stuart, it was just so hard on her. Her only daugh-
ter, all her dreams . . ."

"All of mine, too, sir."

"I know, son, I know. It's just that Emily can't seem to fight it off like you and me. It eats away at her. She'll stare at that picture for hours at a time."

"Does she still blame me?"

Mr. Nash wrinkled his bushy gray eyebrows. "Yes, I guess she does."

"Do you?"

"Stuart, you made my Lisa the happiest girl in this Territory. There was nothing on the face of this earth she ever wanted more than to be the wife of Stuart Brannon. You loved her good. You provided for her. What else could I ask? I believe she was bound to die at the birth of her first child no matter where she lived or who she married. I don't understand that. I never will. Like you, son, I'll carry that pain until the day I die. But I will never blame you."

"Thank you, sir. I appreciate that."

Clearing his throat, Nash continued. "I see you with Miss Reed. Isn't she a dandy? Wouldn't she and Lisa make a pair?"

"If they didn't fight, they would probably redecorate the entire city in a week."

"It's been over two years, hasn't it? About time you started thinking of remarrying?"

"No, sir, I don't believe it's time. It was good to visit. I want you and Mrs. Nash to know that you are still in my prayers."

"She'll get over it, Stuart. Give her more time. Whenever you're in Prescott, stop by the office and see me."

"I'll do that."

It was a quiet Sunday dinner. What with the sermon and the conversation with Mr. Nash, Brannon didn't feel very talkative.

"Mrs. Barton, it was another lovely meal. Please forgive me for being so silent. I guess I've got a lot on my mind."

"It's a pleasure to have you here, Stuart. Next time you come to town, we insist that you eat with us."

"That's a bargain. Now you have to promise that one of these days, you'll get a buggy and ride down to the ranch. I'd love to have the three of you stay with me awhile. Just give me a few weeks to clean up and settle in."

"Yes, well, Harriet has already made some plans. Will you be coming up on the Fourth of July?"

"I'm not sure. It depends on how quickly I can get everything patched up."

Harriet Reed walked him to the door.

"I will miss our evening talks, Stuart Brannon."

"Not nearly as much as I will, Miss Reed. You are very easy to talk to. For a few moments this week it seemed like my life was truly beginning to settle down. It felt peaceful and natural. But . . ."

"But what?"

"Well, the preacher and Mr. Nash reminded me that my life just isn't that way. I hope we have more times to talk, Harriet, but I want to be honest. Stuart Brannon isn't a very good investment. Don't wait for me to get my life settled. You are much too exciting a lady to waste much time with me."

"Mr. Brannon, there is no one on this earth who will tell me how I may or may not waste my time."

"No, Miss Harriet, I don't suppose there is."

He didn't know whether to hug her, shake her hand, or kiss her. So he tipped his hat, turned, and walked down the street toward the livery.

Retrieving El Viento, he spent the early afternoon packing his supplies on the driving horses. Finally, Brannon made one last stop at the doctor's office on his way out of town. A housekeeper whom he had never seen before came to the door.

"Sorry to bother you today. Is the doctor in?"

"Nope. Come back tomorrow."

"Listen, I need to visit Miss Cancino for just a—"

"No visitors today—doctor's orders."

"But I—"

"Are you Brannon?"

"Yes, ma'am."

"Well, why didn't you say so in the first place. Of course you can come in!"

Julie was asleep when he entered the room. Sylvia from the Lucky Dollar sat in a chair, half dozing herself.

"Oh, Mr. Brannon!" Sylvia blurted out. "We thought you left town."

"Not without seeing Miss Julie."

"She's been like this nearly all day. In and out of sleep . . . burning still with fever. Say, did you really kiss her on the lips?"

"I most certainly did."

"I told ya so," Julie rasped, barely opening her eyes.

"I wanted to see you before I rode out to the ranch."

"Have we still got that dance?"

"Are you sure you wouldn't rather have a steak dinner at the nicest place in town?"

"Nope. I laid here all night thinking what a silly sight it will be for some old cowboy like you to go strutting around the dance floor. You can't weasel out of it. You have to dance."

"And you have to get well!"

"Yes, sir. I know I do."

The fresh air of the trail felt good in his face as he rode southeast out of Prescott. When the road eased out of the chaparral and hit the upper levels of the desert, Brannon turned straight east and followed a wagon rut that would lead into the mountains.

FIVE

Ten people traveling the same road see ten different scenes. The trail Brannon took to his ranch would have looked bleak to many a New Englander. No majestic deciduous trees. No lush undergrowth. No frolicking streams.

The old forty-niner would have only seen the granite outcroppings and the promise of color.

The native Indians would have been drawn towards the saguaro blooms perched high in the air, ready for picking with a long pole.

The romanticist would have gazed at the blue and orange wildflowers sprinkled artistically across the hillsides.

Some might notice only the blazing sun and cloudless sky.

Others would search for animal signs along the trail, hoping to put meat on the table.

Stuart Brannon saw only the grass.

Green.

One foot tall.

In some places bunched, thick, vigorous. And in other spots thin, wispy, yellowing.

For a cattleman there was grass . . . and water.

He rode two hard days out of Prescott. He tipped his hat to a lady or two and stopped to jaw with a few men, but mostly he just studied the grass and water.

For him, everything else was an accessory.

Must have had a good wet spring. And most folks in the States

*think Arizona is just sand and cactus! If they ever find out what's
down here . . . it's no wonder the Indians want to keep it all. One
of these days they'll load trains full in Chicago and roll down here
like a flood.*

*'Course they'll have to take a jog around Sunrise Creek. There
won't be any roads through the Triple B Ranch. Not now. Not
then. Not ever.*

At several places along the road Brannon noticed faded handbills that read, "Private Property: Casa Verde Land Corporation."

*Now there you go. The companies are beginning to move in.
Maybe they'll put in a railroad, and we could link up with the S.P.
Then we could ship cows all over the country. If the rail runs fairly
close to the ranch, it might be a good place to put in feed pens.
Ranchers could drive their herds in. We'd hold them in the pens
and fatten them up before shipping them out.*

The road had been no more than two wagon ruts in the grass.
But now, as he turned due east to his place, even the ruts stopped.

"Well, El Viento, we're going home. You've never been there,
but it will be home for a long, long time."

Riding up a long sloping draw, Brannon kept a close eye on the
driving horses who seemed to adapt well to packing a full load.
Reaching the top of the pass, he rested the horses and climbed out
of the saddle. He tied them off to a scrubby cottonwood and
pulled one of the handbills off the trunk of the tree.

"Well, you company boys missed it this time. This is private
property all right. It's part of the Triple B. Next time I'm in Tucson
I'll have to hurrah those surveyors."

Brannon hiked to a large boulder and climbed to the top. It had
always been one of his favorite spots on the ranch. Straight across
to the south was Despoblado Pass. Between where he sat and that
distant pass was all Triple B. It stretched from the flats all along
Sunrise Creek up to Jinete Springs.

From where he sat, Brannon could view 75 percent of the
ranch. At this location he had proposed to Lisa. Here she had
announced her pregnancy. On this spot he had viewed the herd
dead and dying from some unknown disease. And it was at this
point that he had last looked at the ranch.

No cattle roamed his range now. But with the good spring grass, he could not even see the bones of the previous herd. But he could see the house, sheds, and barn.

"Plenty of weeds, but everything more or less standing! With two-foot-thick adobe walls, that house will last a hundred years. Of course, the roof might cave in before that. Maybe a week or two of repairs. Then Fletcher shows up and we . . . what?"

Brannon jumped to his feet. He saw someone leave the bunkhouse and walk towards the barn.

"Squatters!" he barked at the horses.

He galloped the big black horse down the trail towards the ranch, stirring up dust as he rode.

I'm not sneaking up on my own house. I've got my papers in the bag. Probably he's just passing through. I'd do the same thing if I found a deserted place at the end of a long day. I could let him stay until mornin'.

As he rode up to the yard, he noticed more of the "Private Property" signs posted on the outbuildings. He stopped and jerked several of the signs down. He had just reached the barn when a rifle shot ripped into the wood behind him. He slid out of the saddle and had his Winchester cocked and ready to fire by the time he hit the ground.

"Ho! In the bunkhouse!" he yelled.

"This is private property; you'll have to turn around and leave!" someone shouted.

"Private property? You're mighty right about that. I own this place! What are you doing here?"

"Mister," the voice replied, "this valley is owned by the Casa Verde Land Corporation!"

"They might own some land, but not this land," Brannon shouted back, keeping well concealed. Pushing his black hat back, he shoved a couple more shells into the Winchester. "Now, just walk out of there peaceful like, and I'll show you the patent deed."

"Can't do that. I've been hired by Mr. Warren G. Burlingame of San Francisco to protect this property in the name of the C.V.L."

"I don't care who hired you; you've got the wrong place. This is my ranch."

"Mister, I've been here four months. I've fought off Apaches, Yavapais, prospectors, outlaws, and malaria, but I ain't never seen you. Git on yore horse and ride right back out of here!"

"Look, I've got papers on this place. If you don't come out, I'll have to shoot you for trespassing."

"C.V.L. has got papers, too, and you'll be the one shot for trespassing. If you want to discuss a legal claim, go down to the Surveyor-General's office in Tucson. But until I'm instructed differently, you're not coming on this place!"

"Sorry you feel that way. Now I presume you got some identification papers on you. You know—your name, your mama's name, address of where you would like the body shipped, and all that."

This time the shots were not fired above Brannon, but right at him. And only the thick beams at the corner of the barn protected him.

I've got to shoot up my own place in order to get home!

The house was still boarded up. Keeping hidden behind the barn, Brannon pulled the saddle off El Viento and walked the horse to the barn.

"What are you doing out there?"

"Putting my horse in my barn," Brannon shouted.

"You cain't do that!"

Several shots banged harmlessly at the top of the barn.

"I can do it and I'm going to shoot that horse in the corral."

"You cain't do that!"

"Well, you're right. I hate to harm good horseflesh. So I'll just turn him loose and chase him off!"

"You move towards that corral and I'll kill ya, Mister!"

"In that case, I don't have any choice. I'll just shoot the horse!"

"Wait!" the man screamed again. "Put down your rifle and let's talk this out. I can see you don't understand the situation."

"You leave that Winchester against the door, and I'll prop mine on the barn. Then walk out to the courtyard," Brannon called.

"Move away from that barn."

The door to the bunkhouse slowly swung open. A man appeared and set his rifle against the outside of the building and took one step towards Brannon.

He's got nerve.

Brannon leaned his Winchester against the barn and took several slow steps towards the yard. The two men stopped about thirty feet apart. Both packed Colts on their hips, and both held their hands close to their sides.

"You're just a kid!" Brannon complained.

"Mister, the bullet leaves the gun at the same speed no matter how old you are."

Sounds like Stuart Brannon, age eighteen.

"Look, son, I—"

"Don't call me son. Chances are one of us will be dead in the next few minutes. It'll be man-to-man. There ain't no boys here."

"That's fair enough, Mister. But I can't see why you want to die for the sake of a San Francisco company."

"I hired on to do a job. I won't back out of it."

"Would you be interested at all in seeing my papers to the place before you grab for that gun?"

"Whatever papers you have are no longer valid. This is part of the De Palma-Revera Land Grant which was purchased by Mr. Warren G. Burlingame and the Casa Verde Land Corporation."

"No such grant has been approved by Congress."

"Maybe not, but the papers are filed, and they have possession."

"Listen, why don't you get on that horse, ride to San Francisco, and tell Mr. Burlingame that there has been a slight mistake in the survey and that the Triple B Ranch is not part of the grant?"

"Mister, I don't know who you are. You just rode in here and demanded this valley. I don't bluff that easy. If you're itchin' to pull out that revolver, just go ahead."

Brannon looked at the young man's eyes.

He means it. He will give it his best. He won't bluff down.

"Who do you think built that house?"

"Some Mexicans, I guess."

"I built it!"

"Any fool can say that."

Lord, I'm going to have to shoot him!

Brannon glanced around the ranch house.

"If you've been here that long, then you've hiked up to those two piñon pines?"

"Yep."

"Well, did you notice among those weeds two stone grave markers? One reads, 'Lisa B., always in my heart, 12-25-75,' and the other, 'Baby B., went home with mama, 12-25-75.'"

The young man stared for a moment and then spoke. "Anyone can read a marker."

"You saw me ride down off that north mountain."

"It still don't prove anything. Even if this was your place, it ain't now. That's a fact."

"Mister, I told you that because I want you to know why I'm going to shoot you down. That's my wife and my baby buried up there. I'm not going to leave them to you, to Burlingame, or to a corporation. I believe you understand my position."

"And you understand mine. I signed on for a job, and I'm going to do it!"

"Yep, I understand. I was eighteen once."

"I'm twenty!"

"Well, what's your name, son? I do promise to send you home."

About my height . . . a little thin in the shoulders. Probably the kind that can ride eighteen hours a day.

"Earl Howland."

"Well, Earl, if you want to change your mind about this shooting stuff, this would be a good time."

Strong arms, tanned face . . . he's put in more than one hard day's work.

"Look, you'll be the one who's planted today," Howland insisted. "And I'll stick you up there in those piñons if you like. Just what name do you want on that stone?"

"Oh, it will be there someday, Earl. But you won't be the one doing it."

Probably hasn't shaved twice in his life, but he's tough enough to stick it out here by himself.

"And the name?" Howland insisted.

"Brannon. Stuart Brannon."

"You're Stuart Brannon?"

"Yep."

"From Apache Wells? Massacre Meadow? And all of that?"

"Yep."

"Oh . . . great! No one told me this place belonged to Stuart Brannon!"

"I'm telling you."

"Yes, sir . . . well, well . . . I've got a job to do, and I can't back away. I wouldn't be no good to myself if I backed away."

"Earl, I know exactly what you mean. How much are they paying you for this job?"

"Thirty a month plus grub, and a thousand dollar bonus when the claim is settled."

"When did they pay you last?"

"Two months ago."

"Well, don't you think that's a little lax?"

"Someone will be along soon."

"You know, if a man failed to live up to an agreement with me, I'd quit him. Especially if I had a better offer."

"What are you saying?"

"I'm saying you have no obligation to work for free. And I'll offer you forty a month, room and board, and when we drive a herd up from Mexico, I'll give you twenty cows of your own and a bull."

"My own herd?"

"Well, it will be the makin's of one."

"Why should I believe you?"

"Why should you believe Casa Verde Land Corporation?"

"It's either that or draw, ain't it?"

"Those are the only choices I know of."

"You know that they'll just come in here with more men?"

"That's why I need a good man like you on my side."

"How do I know you won't shoot me down anyway?"

"Earl, if I wanted to shoot you, I certainly would have done it before now." With that, Brannon went for his gun. Startled, Howland reached to draw his own, but he hadn't raised it up before Brannon's hammer clicked.

Earl froze with his gun half-drawn.

Brannon resat the hammer and shoved the revolver back into the holster.

"You see, Earl, I'm not going to shoot you."

Howland took a big, deep breath and put his gun back into his holster. "I ain't working for a man who don't pay me. You still hirin'?"

"Yep."

"I'd like the job."

"You got it."

Suddenly a smile broke over Howland's face. "What's the first thing you want me to do?"

"Ride around the ranch and rip down those signs!"

"Yes, sir . . . yes, sir, I'll do that."

For two weeks Brannon and Howland repaired the barn, corrals, and the roof on the house. They pulled the weeds out of the yard, cleaned up the buildings, and repaired broken cupboards and furniture.

Following instructions, Howland had lived in the bunkhouse, leaving the big house for Mr. Burlingame, who as yet hadn't the time to come visit his newly acquired "estate."

For the first several days Brannon tried to get Howland to call him Stuart. On the fourth day he gave up trying. A pattern developed. They sat on the front porch after supper and watched the sun disappear and the stars come out. Most of the conversation centered around Howland pumping Brannon for every detail of every gunfight and exploit.

"Mr. Brannon, this place is looking downright livable."

"It's a start, Earl. I don't know what the future's going to be, but a friend of mine's going to ride in here in a few days. An Englishman by the name of Fletcher—Edwin Fletcher. He'll take one of those rooms in the big house. You're welcome to take the little room at the back of the house, or you can have that bunkhouse all to yourself. Sort of like a place of your own for a while. Which do you want?"

"I'd kind of like to just stay in the bunkhouse . . . if it ain't insultin'."

"Nope. I hope to get a cook out here one of these days. Then we'll enjoy mealtimes better."

"When are we going to go get the cows?"

"Well, I've still got some things to settle here, and I need to write to some folks in Mexico. Then I'm thinking of digging out some catch ponds up at the Jinete Springs and putting in some dams along Sunrise Creek. Maybe that will slow down the flash floods and the disease. Wouldn't hurt to put up some of that new wire fencing across the upper end. Once the cows wander up past the springs, the Apaches will get them for sure."

"Where's the wire for the fence?"

"At the store, I suppose."

"Are you going to town?"

"You're going to town. You need to buy a wagon, plus the supplies on this list. You can drive a team, can't you?"

"Yes, sir," Howland said with a nod. "You want me to go to town by myself?"

"Here's the list; can you read?"

"Oh, yes, sir."

"Well, read through this list and see if you can figure everything out."

For several minutes Howland studied the list.

"Well, sir . . . I think I got it all . . . except this here last item. Is that something ya eat?"

Brannon laughed. "*The Iliad and the Odyssey?* It's a book, Earl! I read it years ago, but I need to study up on it. Go see Tom Weedin over at *The Enterprise*. He'll know if there's a copy of it in town. You can head out first thing in the morning. I'll give you some money to get the goods."

Howland pulled off his dusty brown hat and spun it around on his finger. Then he jammed it back on his sandy colored hair and stood to his feet.

"Mr. Brannon, how do you know I won't just ride on out of here with your money and never come back?"

"'Cause you would die of shame within two days if you did that."

A big wide grin broke across Howland's face.

"Yeah . . . but how did you know that?"

"Because honesty and integrity show on a man. You can only survive out here in this rough country if you learn to read folks well."

"So you read me, did ya?"

"Well . . . let me guess." Brannon leaned his chair back against the wall and tugged off his boots. "Your mama raised you on the Good Book, and your daddy taught you to work hard. They must have both died, or you'd be with them. You like being alone—riding the mountains . . . anything from the back of a horse . . . feel awkward around the ladies . . . and figure that keepin' your word to God and man is just about the most important thing on earth."

Brannon dumped a little sand out of his boots and then propped his feet up on the rail. "How am I doin' so far?"

"You could read all of that?"

"All I got to do is remember when I was eighteen."

"Twenty," Howland corrected, "but you were wrong about my mama. She's still alive. Lives with my older brother in Louisiana." He walked over and leaned against a horse rail. "Mr. Brannon, I'd like to buy a new pair of trousers."

"And a new shirt."

"Yes, sir. You know, it will take me a while to drive a team back up here."

"I'm not going anyplace. Remember, this is my home."

"Yes, sir . . . well, you can count on me."

"I am, Earl. I surely am."

The next morning Howland saddled up and rode south leading the team of horses. Brannon watched from the barn until he crested Despoblado Pass.

Lord . . . young Earl is a good working boy. Take care of him. This country needs a lot more Earls.

Brannon rode El Viento up the mountain to the Jinete Springs. Above them the rocks and trees alternated as barriers. No easy riding. He scouted a possible fence line. He figured that one hundred posts should make an effective barricade.

He took his time riding back to the ranch house, stopped at several places along Sunrise Creek to check out possible holding ponds. His nooner consisted of some jerky, creek water, and a short nap. Near sunset he rode back down toward the barn and house. His mind was engineering a ranch water supply. His rifle was still in the scabbard, his Colt tucked into his belt.

It was a dumb stunt.

Brannon knew better.

He was within sight of the house when he finally looked up and discovered three extra horses turned out in his corral.

Visitors?

Here I am in the clear already!

They've surely spotted me. I can't hide. Nice work, Brannon! Why not just wear a "shoot me" sign around your neck! Did they come from the south or the north? What about Earl?

Brannon slipped his Colt from the holster and held it inside his jacket.

If they turned the horses out, they plan on stayin'.

He spotted one man with a rifle standing in the barn door. Another man, hand on his hip, stood in the open doorway of the house.

"Mister, are you lost?" the one at the barn called.

"Did you drift in from the high country? Maybe you seen Howland up there?" the other man hollered.

They haven't seen Earl . . . and there's another one somewhere.

He pulled up by the house and considered dismounting next to a post for protection from the man with the rifle.

"Keep riding, Mister! You ain't stopping here!"

From the back of the house he heard a third voice shout, "Eeuu-wee, Todd, you ought to come look at this kitchen. Earl has it polished up like a widah lady's!"

The voice was familiar, but Brannon couldn't place it.

"We got a visitor out here, Riley!"

Then Brannon remembered. The man with the gun at the Lucky Dollar!

"Well, chase him off the . . . Brannon?" he shouted, dropping a biscuit and grabbing for his revolver.

Brannon dove from El Viento and shot at the same time.

A blast from the rifle slammed against the adobe wall of the house above his head, and the other man at the door shot wild. Brannon's hurried shot missed both men at the door and ripped through the bottom hinge.

The two men bolted back inside the house, and El Viento sprinted up the road towards the high end of the ranch. Brannon rolled behind the side of the house to get out of range of the rifle, but his right foot caught a piercing burst of heat. He knew he'd been hit. Blood seeped through a hole ripped in his boot as he crawled out of the line of fire.

There's no cover around here! If they rush me, it'll be tough to take all three!

Three chollas sprawled along the side of the house, and Brannon rolled back among the drooping cactus. He was facing the barn. Suddenly he spun his head around to the east just as Riley, the man from the Lucky Dollar, stepped away from the back of the house and raised his gun.

Brannon's first shot caught the man in the stomach. He fired back hitting the cholla near Brannon's head. A piece of cholla propelled into his face like needles stuck in a pincushion.

Brannon screamed and grabbed at the cactus.

The man staggered back, and Brannon's second shot dropped him to the ground. Brannon dragged himself to the back of the house and through the door. He shut it softly.

"Riley's got him!"

"Cover me, Rawnie."

The man with the rifle walked slowly across the yard with the gun still at his shoulder. "See anything?" he called.

With revolver cocked, the first man rounded the corner of the house.

"It's Riley!"

"Is he dead?"

"Yeah."

"Where's that drifter? I know I shot him in the leg. Look at all this blood!"

"It leads towards the back door. Brannon must be in the house!" Todd replied.

"Brannon? Stuart Brannon?"

"That's what Riley called out when he came out the front door."

Rawnie dove low against the side of the house, pulling Todd with him. "Stay down! If that's Brannon, we're in for a fight."

"But there's two of us."

"Yeah . . . there used to be three, remember?"

"He's wounded."

"He made it back into the house, didn't he?"

"What are we going to do?"

"We'll need some help!"

"You mean Jedel and the boys?"

"Yep. Hank Jedel is the only one in the Territory who says he can face down Stuart Brannon."

"So we're just going to ride out of here?"

"You want to go into this house and face Brannon? You heard what they was sayin' about him in Prescott."

"But he's wounded, ain't he?"

"I don't want to face him even if he's dead."

"How are we going to get to the barn and the horses?"

"Maybe he's covering the back door. He cain't be both places at the same time."

"Well . . . I'll go straight to the barn for the saddles and you tear off for the corrals."

"Now?"

"Now!"

Both men kept low and ran across the yard.

There was no gunfire.

Within moments they had saddled up and were sprinting up the trail.

Brannon did not see their exit. He had managed to drag himself through the back door, across the pantry, and into the kitchen. His right boot was full of blood, and his face streamed red. He had pulled himself to a corner of the room, behind the cook stove, where he could watch both doors at once.

Then he waited for the attack.

Moments later he thought he heard a couple of horses pull out for the north trail. Dragging himself into the living room, he reared up to look through the unshuttered window and saw their dust already high on the trail.

Lord, this is bad—real bad.

Crawling back to the kitchen, he grabbed a carving knife and cut his boot off his foot. He wrapped the wound with several tea towels to stop the bleeding. The bullet had gone through his foot and lodged in the leather heel.

"I've got to clean up this mess," he mumbled.

Finding another rag, he pulled himself up to the kitchen pump and cranked up a little water. Then turning towards the table, he tried to put some weight on his wounded foot.

He collapsed to the wooden floor.

This time he didn't move again.

S I X

When Brannon came to, the shooting pain in his right foot was equaled by fire in his face and forehead. He struggled to his hands and knees, but could go no further in the now dark kitchen.

Lisa? She needs me! I can't track mud across the floor. Where's the bedroom? I need a lantern . . . hurry! Don't let her down. If I don't get there soon, she'll . . . hang on, babe . . . hang on. I'll be there!

Brannon stumbled across the wet rag he had grabbed to clean the floor. He squeezed it to his forehead.

Everett? They shot Everett! No! They can't do that! Where's my Winchester? Still on Sage . . . Sage, old boy . . . no, no, they shot Sage. Why, Lord, why did they have to shoot Sage?

Julie's dying. She's dying. It's crazy. They need me. Where's my horse? Where's my horse! Lisa! I'm here now. It's OK. Everything will be all right, honey.

Mrs. Nash . . . I did everything I could . . . my God, I did everything I could!

Elizabeth is lost. The brave little warrior . . . where's the little warrior? I can't see anything.

Crawling on his hands and knees Brannon stumbled into the bedroom and pulled himself onto the bed. He wrapped the wet rag around his head. His hand brushed against the cactus thorns still embedded in his cheek.

Bees! Swarms of bees! Water. I need water. Where's the river?

We'll get you well, Lisa. You rest up.
I can't tell her, Lord. I can't tell her. I can't . . .
Lisa . . . honey, the baby's . . . he's dead . . . my, God, he's dead!
Violent men build a violent society! I'm not a violent man! Do
you hear me? I am not a violent man!

When Brannon woke up, someone was rubbing a wet rag across his forehead.

Yellow hair. Green eyes. Troubled eyes. Ribbon in her hair.
Green dress. A good woman. A real good woman . . . and a man.
Black vest. Gray hair.

Brannon tried to raise his head.

"So you are alive!" The woman was brushing his hair out of his eyes.

"Judge Quilici? Sage? What's . . ."

"Lay back down. Let's start from the top."

"Where's Lisa? Where's—"

"Stuart!" Sage Quilici interrupted. "Stuart, you've been shot!"

Brannon sat straight up in bed.

"What day is it?"

"Sunday." Mrs. Quilici pushed him back down on the pillow. "When did you get shot?"

"Last night . . . I think . . . or maybe it was the night before. What are you two doing here?"

"Do you need a drink of water?"

"Yeah."

Mrs. Quilici brought him a cup a water and helped him take a drink. Then it was the judge who spoke. "Last evening Earl Howland, one of the C.V.L. men, rode into our ranch and said he was now working for you. Well, we let him bunk in the barn. So this morning after the services, we decided—"

"Services? A church? There's a church here now?"

"Not yet," Sage Quilici explained. "But several of the neighbors have been riding to our place when the weather's good. We're thinking of building a church by the cottonwood grove between your place and ours. We figure if we have a building, maybe we can get a circuit preacher from Prescott to come out."

"Anyway," the judge continued, "we wanted to welcome you

back. When we got here, we found one horse in the corral, a big black saddled up and wandering around the yard, a dead man just outside your back door, and you ranting and raving in the bed."

"He was one of the C.V.L. Collectors, wasn't he?" she asked.

"Yeah, I guess that's what you call them. They were in my house and jumped me when I rode back down out of the mountains. Judge, what's this Burlingame Land Grant all about?"

"Well, besides owning half of San Francisco, he seems to be trying to get half of Arizona. Burlingame's lawyers claim that he purchased a valid Spanish land grant. He doesn't want people to move in on the land until Congress settles the issue."

"He doesn't have any grant on this property. Who believes this land grant stuff anyway?"

"Arizona Mining Corporation, for one."

"What?"

"Yeah, they looked at his papers and gave him a $50,000 retainer for the right to continued exploration."

"Arizona Mining?"

"Yes. So every few months Burlingame's agents come by to collect rent. That's why we call them the Collectors."

"Before the matter's settled?"

"He says he'll issue long-term leases only to those who honor the grant now. He vows to evict everyone else."

"And they're falling for that?"

"Some are."

"And you two?"

"So far they've been skipping over us."

"That's because the judge has some influential friends in San Francisco. But if Burlingame wins his case, we'll all be out of here," Mrs. Quilici reported.

"This De Palma-Revera Land Grant. We were all told that was just an old legend."

"It is," the judge insisted. "That's why this thing is a crock! De Palma-Revera was run out of Santa Fe by the governor over a hundred years ago. Now the C.V.L.'s claiming the same governor granted him 117,000 acres of Arizona land!"

"Well, they aren't getting my ranch!"

Mrs. Quilici glared down at his injured foot. "It looks like they almost did."

"Yeah . . . isn't that beautiful?"

"Sage," the judge added, "how about stirring Brannon up a little supper? I need to get things put up outside. Whose horse is in the corral?"

"The dead man's."

"And how about the big black?"

"That's mine. If you can catch him, unsaddle him and put him in the corral."

"What happened to my pony?" Mrs. Quilici called from the kitchen.

"I called him Sage after you, you know. He took a bullet up in Colorado."

"And the dead man?" the judge asked.

"Bury him . . . but not by Lisa and the baby. Anywhere behind the barn."

Brannon lay on his back as the Quilicis straightened the house and yard. They were the first folks he had befriended in Arizona. Although more than seven miles away, they were his nearest neighbors. They had helped him stake off the ranch and file the papers. They had helped him build the house and the barn. They had helped him bury Lisa and the baby.

Brannon was sitting up in bed when Mrs. Quilici brought him some apple flapjacks and beef-carrot stew. She could outride, outrope, and outcook any woman in Arizona.

"Stuart, you don't have many supplies around here."

"That's what Howland's going for."

"Well, there should be enough of this stew for a couple days. After that, it's pretty bleak. How's your face?"

"Feels like a porcupine backed into me."

"The judge and I pulled out the thorns while you were still ranting, but it does look puffy. I washed up that foot and put some clean bandages on it, but you better keep a close eye on it. The wound looks clean so far, but I'm not sure when you'll be able to walk on it."

The judge joined them for supper. His face was as dark and

tough as an old saddle, and the ragged gray hair poked out from under his hat. He was covered with road dust. Yet to Brannon he always looked and acted like a judge.

"Stuart, I don't suppose you'd consider letting me load you up on that pony to ride back to our place for a few days."

"You know I can't do that."

"Yeah . . . well, we'll have to pull out and make it back before dark, or the boys on the ranch will send a posse out after us. I'll send a rider to check on you tomorrow."

"He can bring a few things to eat," Sage Quilici added.

"Much obliged. I think that fever broke, and I'll be able to get around a little."

"Not on that foot, you won't," she warned. "Don't plan on it being very useful for a couple of months."

"I brought your Winchester and saddlebags in and laid them against the front door," the judge reported. "If these were C.V.L. men, you will hear from them again. Hank Jedel is their leader."

"Jedel? Me and Sheriff Rupert pinned him down in Black Canyon. Remember that? Didn't he get a term in A.T.P. for killing a stagecoach driver?"

"That was about the time you lit out for Colorado. Jedel was never convicted. The main witness disappeared. So now he ramrods for C.V.L. and headquarters out of Tucson. You can imagine the kind of men he hires. Lots of folks change their mind in a hurry about paying that extortion money as rent on their own property. As soon as you're up to it, you should ride down to the Surveyor-General's office and file a complaint. It seems to help if you have a formal protest."

"Thanks. I'll wait for Howland and Fletcher to show and then try to do that. I'll stop by your ranch on my way down."

"Fletcher?" she asked.

"An Englishman. Friend of mine who's going into the cattle business with me."

"You sure you're going to be all right?"

"For the first time in over two years I'm sitting in my own home. I'm going to be fine."

He wanted to see them to the door, but didn't bother trying.

Sometime midway through the next day Stuart Brannon decided he was not going to die. Not that he had actually thought he was. He had just reached his absolute limits for staying in bed.

He hopped about the house, first to the living room to look out at the barn and horses, then to the kitchen for fresh water and bandages. His face swelled, one eye almost shut; plus a one-week beard gave him the grizzled "old-prospector" look.

He tried washing his foot wound. The pain was just as great, but it looked better. He wrapped it as tight as his tolerance would allow. Then he pulled on his left boot and jabbed his hat on his head.

No reason to comb my hair. Brannon, you disguise your handsome features well! If I don't shoot 'em, I can scare 'em off.

In the pantry he found a five-foot piece of shelving to use for a crutch. His Winchester made a cane. He staggered across the yard towards the barn. When he reached the door, he was so worn out that he considered spending the night there.

Catching his breath, he hobbled over to the corral and checked the water trough. It still held at least ten gallons. Then he pulled down a little hay for the two animals.

Again he hobbled back to the barn and rested for a few minutes.

He didn't go to sleep.

He was just resting his eyes.

Still, the voices startled him.

"Ho! In the house! Mr. Brannon? Judge Quilici sent us over with supplies!"

"Mr. Brannon, are you inside?"

Struggling to his feet, Brannon searched for his shelving crutch and shuffled out of the barn.

"Over here, boys. I was feedin' the horses!"

"That's Stuart Brannon?" he heard one of Quilici's cowhands mumble.

"Shh!" the *vaquero* with him replied.

"But . . . but he's an old man! I . . . I thought, you know . . . that Brannon was still in his prime!"

"Mister Brannon, I'm Ignacio Fernandez, and this talkative

compadre is Floyd. Judge Quilici sent us over to see how you are doing. Missus sent some food too. Floyd, take that grub sack into the house."

Floyd swung out of the saddle and began to untie the supplies.

"Are you really Stuart Brannon?"

"I seem to get asked that a lot lately. Well, Floyd, just remember it's not the years but the miles that age a man. And I want to tell you boys, I've just been down some mighty rough miles."

"Judge said you gunned down one of the C.V.L. Collectors."

"Some guy named Riley, I think."

"You shot Riley?" Floyd gasped.

"Yeah, three of them jumped me and—"

"Three of them?"

"Yeah."

"Too bad you didn't lead down Jedel. He's the worst of them."

"Jedel? He wasn't with them."

"Yeah, I heard he was headed to Santa Fe. Mr. Brannon, the judge said we should do any chores you need," Fernandez offered. "Can we pull down some hay, or anything?"

"Much obliged. The hay would help, and if you'd carry a few buckets of water for that trough. I don't think I'll be ready to dance on this foot for a while."

The men finished the chores and then came back over to Brannon who was sitting out in front of the house. They mounted up and were just ready to leave when the one named Floyd rode a little closer.

"Mr. Brannon . . . I'm sorry about them words I spoke. I should just keep my mouth shut."

"No harm done, Floyd. I look a might frightful."

"I was wondering if you had some advice you could give me, you know, you being a veteran gunman and me just starting out."

Brannon fought to keep from laughing.

"Floyd, don't ever, ever lay in a patch of cholla when you're in the midst of a gun battle."

"Eh . . . no, sir, I won't. I won't. Thank you, sir."

Within three dusty minutes both men were out of sight.

Harriet stepped out on the front porch and glanced down the street towards the courthouse. She couldn't see her brother-in-law, so she walked back inside, straightened the umbrellas near the hall closet, and ascended the staircase slowly, dragging her hanky slowly up the bannister as she went.

Remember boarding school days of hiding under the comforter and giggling about a handsome knight on a white horse that carries us off? We set such high standards of character and bravery and handsomeness that no man could expect to live up to it. However, my dear, it just might be that my knight has arrived (riding a black horse, which is not a serious flaw in the scheme of things).

After several days visiting with him, I was able to write three chapters last week! Can you imagine! His life is like a novel, with a new adventure each day.

That does seem to validate all those years of prayers.

Anyway, the point being, Mr. Barton mentioned yesterday evening that it looked as if he and several others would need to go to Phoenix (a hot, sticky little farm town on the Salt River). He suggested that Gwen and I could come along and that we should stop by and see Mr. Brannon as long as we were going near there. I packed a few things this morning just in case we needed to slip away quickly, but as it turned out, Nelson hasn't returned since early this morning. If you do not hear from me for a while, it will be because I'm stranded on a ranch in the middle of Arizona Territory.

(Now if you think I said all of that just to make you jealous, you are absolutely right!)

Perhaps by the next letter I will have something truly momentous to write.

Give my best to Rachel.

> Affectionately yours,
> Miss Harriet Reed

She didn't see her brother-in-law until they all gathered at the supper table.

"It has taken me all day to make the arrangements! We will be leaving in the morning for Phoenix!"

"Wonderful!" Harriet cried.

"Who will be going with us?" Gwendolyn probed.

"Well, that's the interesting part. It started out simply as a land matter. I was going to take two of the men from the office and a translator."

"Five of us in one coach?" Gwendolyn asked.

"Well, it's more complicated than that. I saw Captain Wells at dinner, and he said the army wanted to send a small contingent of men down to that area and would be happy to ride along with us as escorts."

"That does sound safe."

"Oh, it gets even more complicated. I ran across Dr. Levine at the courthouse, and when I told him about our trip, he asked if we had room to transport one of his patients to Phoenix. They have opened a sanitarium in the mountains near there, and this young woman needs some rehabilitation."

"The Cancino woman?"

"Was that the one who got shot?"

"Yes."

"Yes . . . that's her. Well, of course it's our Christian duty to help out."

Harriet nodded politely and murmured, "Naturally. Is Miss Cancino well enough to make such an arduous journey?"

"Dr. Levine believes so. And I understand the young lady was quite delighted at the prospect of going to Phoenix."

"Undoubtedly it has nothing to do with stopping at Brannon's ranch," Harriet grumbled under her breath. "So we're all descending upon Mr. Brannon?"

"Well," Barton responded, "yes, but I have arranged supplies so that we won't be a burden."

"Well, just how many people are going to be in our party?"

"Two carriages, twelve soldiers. Quite an adventure, wouldn't you say?"

"Yes, indeed." Harriet flashed her patented smile of agreement.

After supper Harriet helped clear the table and then excused herself and retired to her room.

So young Miss Julie Cancino will be traveling with us?

She opened her trunk and began to rethink her wardrobe.

It was almost 9:00 A.M. the next morning when two carriages rolled up to the two-story Victorian house. Mr. Barton had gone out several hours earlier to make the final arrangements. From her vantage point in the front window, Harriet watched him hop out of the front carriage and bound up the steps.

"All right, ladies, let's load up. Mr. Gonzales is driving our carriage, Gwendolyn. And Mr. Harvey, the second. Harriet, I believe it might be helpful if you rode in that one with Miss Cancino. She might need some assistance from time to time."

"Certainly." Carrying an unopened parasol, she swooped down off the steps and into the carriage.

"Well, you must be young Julie." *You would think that even a waitress in a cafe would wear something a bit more modest. Of course, she might not have anything else.*

"And you must be Miss Reed! It's very nice to meet you. I've been wanting to ask you a question."

"Please, go ahead."

"Are you going to marry Stuart Brannon or not?"

Harriet Reed coughed and raised her gloved hand to cover her mouth. "What?"

"Oh, you know how people talk around town. They say you're sweet on Brannon. Now I wouldn't blame you if you were. He's probably the most famous man I ever kissed."

I suppose I could just push her out of the wagon if we roll by a steep cliff.

"I tell you what, Miss Cancino—"

"Please call me Julie. But don't ever call me 'young Julie.'"

"Yes, and you must call me Harriet. Well, Julie . . . what's it going to be? Shall be fight and snipe this whole trip, or try to be friends?"

"Well, I had it all planned to fight and snipe, but . . . how about a little truce? You stop calling me 'young Julie,' and I won't mention kissing Stuart Brannon. I've got a feeling we might as well be honest with each other. I know exactly what you think of me, and you undoubtedly know what I think of you."

"Julie, you're probably the most forward woman I've met in a long time." Then Harriet paused for a moment. "And I think I like that."

Miss Cancino brushed her hair back. "Let's start over!"

"And how do we do that?"

"Harriet, that is a beautiful dress."

"Thank you, Julie, and might I add quite honestly that if I had the nerve, I'd love to wear a dress like yours."

Suddenly the carriage jolted forward, and the journey began.

Near the south side of Prescott, Sergeant Cloverdale and his platoon joined the carriages. The party rattled down the dusty road out of the mountains.

Lord, if I can't keep him away from some dining hall waitress, well, I should just find that out right now. I don't want to be bitter, jealous, or vindictive.

By noon Miss Reed and Miss Cancino were visiting like old neighbors, and by the first evening Harriet treated Julie like a younger sister.

"You look rather pale," she cautioned.

"I haven't been out much; I am more tired than I thought," Cancino replied. "Harriet, may I stay in your tent? I might need some extra help, and I don't know any of these others."

"I insist. You should really lie down as soon as the cots are drawn up. I'll bring you some supper." Then she turned to the driver. "Mr. Harvey, you will need to assist Miss Cancino . . . and please be very careful."

Buzzing around through camp, Harriet soon had most of it organized, especially the care and feeding of Miss Julie Cancino.

That evening, after Harriet had prayed for the two of them, Miss Cancino spoke up.

"You know . . . this morning I couldn't tell whether I wanted to shoot you or rip your eyes out. And tonight I just want to hug you and say thanks. How in the world am I ever going to compete with the likes of you? If Brannon is so stupid as to ignore you, I don't think I want him!"

"Julie, don't think too lightly of yourself. You're a beautiful woman . . . who's had to work hard. That's exactly the kind of woman who fits out on a ranch. Look at these weak, pale hands of mine. Hardly the look of a rancher's wife."

"Thanks, I appreciate that, but I'm just kidding myself anyway. I wouldn't be of no help on a ranch . . . or anywhere what with me being like this!"

"Miss Cancino, don't you start feeling sorry for yourself. The doctor said the physical therapy and mineral baths should do you a world of good."

"Yeah, but I don't need a world of good," Julie said with a sigh. "I need a miracle."

"Well, then, we shall just ask the Lord for a miracle!"

Midway through the next morning it was obvious to all that Miss Cancino's strength was failing. They continually slowed the carriage to avoid jolting her. And when they turned off the main trail to circle back into the hills towards Brannon's ranch, the pace slowed even more. Unable to sit up, she lay across Harriet Reed's lap for most of the afternoon.

After leading his troops up into the mountains on an exploratory excursion, Sergeant Cloverdale rejoined the carriages by midafternoon.

"The Triple B should be not more than ten or twelve miles up the road," he reported.

"I would hardly call this goat trail a road," Gwendolyn Barton replied.

"Should we try to press on tonight? Miss Cancino is having a rather rough time of it," Nelson Barton asked.

The sergeant tipped his hat at the women. "I don't think any of us are in such a hurry as to jeopardize her health. Let's camp over by the cottonwoods."

This time two of the men carried Julie to the tent, and Harriet Reed helped her to bed.

"I think it's because the medicine wore off," Julie reported. "The doctor had been giving me some laudanum for the pain, but

I told him I didn't want to take it anymore. I don't think I'm any worse. I can just feel the pain more."

"Perhaps some sleep will help. I heard the men say we should be reaching Brannon's before noon tomorrow."

"You know what's funny, Harriet?"

"What?"

"Well, yesterday morning I was ready to claw your eyes out to get Stuart Brannon for myself."

"And now?"

"Now I'd trade him straight across for a painless night's sleep."

"And me?"

"Harriet, that's the trouble with you. You're just too nice to hate!"

"Can I rub your shoulders?"

"Please."

Lord, Julie is hurting so bad. This would be a very good time for a miracle of some sort.

Within fifteen minutes the miracle came.

Julie Cancino fell sound asleep.

The whole party was excited as they broke camp the next morning. Each of them had a reason for wanting to see Stuart Brannon, and the prospect of only a few hours' ride refreshed them all.

Miss Cancino seemed especially pert. "Harriet, you can't believe what a difference a good night's sleep made. I think that's the first solid sleep I've had in two weeks."

"I know." Harriet settled down in the carriage next to Julie.

"How did you know?"

"You snored."

"No . . . oh, no . . . how embarrassing!"

"I will never tell a soul—except . . ."

"Except who?"

"Oh . . . except for a certain Mr. Brannon. It's the kind of thing I think he should know."

"What!" Julie shrieked. "You do that and I'll . . . I'll burn you at the stake!"

Both women laughed.

"I'm glad to see you're feeling better," Reed commented.

"Tell me the truth, Harriet; do I look frightful?"

"Julie, I doubt if there has ever been a day in your life that you didn't look beautiful. I had to shout to keep those soldiers from fighting over who would assist you to the carriage."

"Really?"

"Yes, it's disgusting, isn't it?"

They giggled their way down the road for the next two hours.

Brannon spent the morning trying to carry water to the horse trough.

I always said I'd set a pump by the barn. There's no reason not to dig another well. It would save a lot of work, especially for cripples.

Finally, he left his Winchester leaning against the barn and hopped across the yard with a wooden bucket half full of water in one hand and his piece of shelving under the other armpit. It took him ten grueling trips to fill the trough.

By the time he finished, he was ringing wet with sweat. Finally, he perched himself on the side of the water trough and splashed water on his face. The water stung the infected places left by the cactus needles, but he splashed on more and more.

Then he just tossed his hat to the ground and dunked his whole body from the waist up, shirt and all, into the water. As he raised up, he shook the water off his head like a dog.

The sound of hoofbeats caused him to whip around to the north. The dust clouds of many riders so startled him that he jumped to his feet to retrieve the rifle. Immediately pain shot through his right foot, and he collapsed into the dirt of the corral.

The dirt turned to mud as he dragged himself toward the barn. Pulling himself inside, he leaned against the barely open door and cocked his Winchester.

It took almost twenty minutes for the slow-moving procession to reach his house and roll into his yard.

Cloverdale? The Bartons? Harriet? Miss Julie?

His handy crutch board having been left by the trough, Brannon hopped out into the yard using his rifle for a cane.

"Yo! You by the barn," Nelson Barton called out, "have you seen Mr. Stuart Brannon around?"

Brannon glanced down at the water and mud still dripping.

For a split second he thought about saying, *No. You've got the wrong ranch!*

SEVEN

Brannon hobbled a few steps forward and promptly fell flat on his face. The sergeant rode over to him.

"Well, don't just sit there on your McClellan, Cloverdale. Get down here and help me up!" Brannon muttered.

"Brannon?" Then he turned to the others and shouted, "It's Brannon!"

"I wasn't exactly expecting company."

"What happened?" the sergeant pressed.

"Are you going to get down here and help me, or do I have to shoot that horse out from under you?"

For the next half hour there was confusion as Brannon tried to clean up, explain his circumstances, and offer hospitality to the entire party. With Private Jenner supporting his right side, he finally emerged from the house, fairly clean and almost recognizable. Everyone stopped their unloading and huddled around him.

"Look, I took a bullet in the foot and a piece of cholla in the face. I had to fight my way back onto my own ranch, was later jumped by three men, and spent a couple days delirious with fever. Other than that, it's been pretty uneventful."

After catching up on their news, he began to give a few orders. "Sergeant, you and your men can set up camp at the barn. Mr. and Mrs. Barton, Miss Reed, and Miss Cancino will take the house. And, you drivers, you'll be with me in the bunkhouse."

"Oh, we couldn't push you out of your home—" Mrs. Barton started to protest.

"You don't have any choice, ma'am. Since this is my ranch, you'll have to take my hospitality."

Julie Cancino still sat in the carriage. When he finished, he hobbled over to her.

"Miss Julie, I'm thrilled to see you out and around. I don't think anything has cheered me up more than sighting you in that carriage. I still can't believe it!"

"Now, Stuart, you didn't think I was the kind of girl you could just kiss and leave, did you?"

"Well, I hope you don't want that dance very soon. Hop and fall down seem to be the only things I do well. Can I help you down?"

"I wish," she said looking into Brannon's eyes, "I wish I could bounce out of here and be of some help to you. But I . . . I mean, I can't yet . . . you see, there's just no . . . ." She took a deep breath and glanced helplessly at Harriet Reed.

"Stuart," Harriet replied, "Julie is unable to move either of her legs. That's why she's going to the sanitarium near Phoenix. There's a good chance it will help."

Brannon sighed. "Don't we make a fine pair?"

Within an hour, Harriet Reed had the whole party organized and operating with efficiency. She and her sister settled their belongings in the house and began fixing dinner. Brannon was seated with his foot in the air on a chair on the front porch. Next to him sat Nelson Barton, and on the other side of the doorway, wrapped in a light quilt with her eyes closed, sat Julie Cancino.

After some time, Sergeant Cloverdale approached.

"Now, Sergeant, exactly how did Mr. Barton rate a twelve-man escort?"

"We got a report that a band of Apaches raided a ranch east of here. One of the leaders was a man called Two Slash. It seems he has two deep cuts in his forearms."

"The same band that jumped you?"

"Perhaps . . . that's why we rode down here. Have you seen any sign of Indians?"

"Only at the far end of the ranch, near Jinete Springs. They come out of the rocks and trees to borrow a little water from time to time."

"Is that east of here?"

"Straight up the mountain slope. Just follow Sunrise Creek."

"How far is it?"

"About half a day's ride."

"Maybe we'll ride up there tomorrow and scout around."

"Good. Then the others can stay here until you return. You aren't in a hurry to move on, are you?" he asked Barton.

"In a hurry? I think Harriet's moved us in permanent!"

By early evening the Triple B looked more like a town than a ranch. The soldiers set up their tents across from the bunkhouse. Men milled around the barn, taking turns riding El Viento, who never grew tired of racing down the trail. Several worked at Brannon's blacksmith shop where Barton's drivers repaired one of the carriages.

Brannon managed to pull himself onto the top rail of the corral and watch all the action. The lantern cast shadows of the women at work in the house.

Well, babe, would you look at this? Our place packed with people. Someday, we said, someday there will be neighbors, and friends, and total strangers just stopping by. Laughing, singing, working, playing . . . and . . . and little kids running through the yard. But there are no kids.

I miss you, Lisa. I really miss you.

"Mr. Brannon?"

Private Jenner stood near the corral.

"Mr. Brannon, would you like some help getting back to the house?"

"Jenner, if you've got the time, I'd like your help getting up to those two piñon pines on that far rim."

"I got time. What's up there?"

"A couple of good friends."

He and Jenner didn't say much until they reached the trees.

"It's a grave!"

"Two of them. My wife and a son."

"Sorry, sir. Did the Indians get them?"

"Nope. Childbirth. Jenner, would you mind giving me a half hour and then coming back for me?"

"No, sir." He turned on his heels and moseyed back down the sloping hill.

Brannon scooted over to the base of one of the trees and leaned his back against it. Picking up small pebbles, he began tossing them towards the newly cleaned grave sites.

For over two years I've been chasing all over this country. I know I should have come back sooner. It's just that one thing led to another . . . and I was scared.

Scared that I couldn't face the place without you.

Afraid to come back.

Afraid not to come back.

It's not the same.

At least there are voices tonight. Voices and laughter and songs. Of course, they're the wrong voices and laughter and songs.

I know what you're sayin' . . . two years is long enough.

Well, Lisa honey, I thought it would be.

But every woman's smile makes me miss you all the more. And the closer I get to them, the more my mind drifts to you. There's two of them down there that . . . they don't know me very well. But they think they do. I know which one you would pick.

"Stick with Miss Harriet. She'll make you governor someday!" You know I've heard that line before.

"That Miss Lisa—she brings out the best in you, boy. If you let her, she'll put you in that big mansion in Prescott."

You would have been the best of friends . . . or the worst of enemies.

But don't overlook Miss Julie's type. When she regains her strength . . . she'd make a ranch wife. She's a stander, too. She'd pull calves, shoot coyotes, mend fences, and raise a yard full of kids, and never complain. She'd run the ranch when I was away and never gripe about the mud on my boots. All she wants is someone to love her.

But it's not me.

Lisa, I can't make 'em happy. I can't even make me happy. The only good thing that's happened lately was this crazy land grant claim on the ranch. Now I've got a reason for hanging on . . . a reason for fighting them.

Don't get me wrong.

It feels good to be home.

Real good.

Jenner came riding up to the trees, leading El Viento.

"You up to a ride?"

"Yeah, I suppose I could give it a try." Using the tree for a prop, he pulled himself up. "Bring him around by these rocks."

With a hard yank on the horn and a leap, Brannon flung his right leg over the saddle and pulled himself up. Jenner handed him the reins.

"Mr. Brannon, the sergeant says you're one of the best Indian fighters in Arizona. Now I don't aim to be an Indian fighter, but I would like to stay alive. What makes a man a good Indian fighter?"

"Well . . . to tell you the truth, Jenner, I never thought about it much. But I guess I would say, first thing is to try to avoid every fight you can. Make friends with them, avoid them, back away, or whatever it takes. Don't look for fights.

"Second, never, ever underestimate their strength, intelligence, and especially their courage. The men who came out here to fight 'dumb' Indians are all dead.

"And then, third, hit them hard with everything you have as quick as you can. They understand and respect strength and bravery. You've got to show them what you have right from the beginning. I hear you're riding up in those eastern mountains tomorrow."

"Yes, sir, that's what the sergeant says."

"Why don't you ask him if a civilian rancher could ride along just as a scout or something? Just up to the springs or so. I've got company to entertain."

"Do you mean that, sir?"

"Jenner, you don't have to call me sir."

"No . . . Mr. Brannon, you're right. I'll go check with the

sergeant!" And he spurred his horse on down the slope to the ranch.

Before he hobbled over to the house, Brannon had checked in with Sergeant Cloverdale and agreed to ride out with them in the morning. He ate supper in the house with the Bartons, Miss Reed, and Miss Cancino.

"Listen, folks, I hope I'm not too poor a host, but I'm going to ride up the ranch a ways with the troops in the morning."

"Do you feel up to it?" Mr. Barton asked.

"Well, that's what I thought I'd find out. I know that country up there and figured I could guide them."

"When will you be back?" Reed asked.

"By evenin' . . . that is, if you all promise to stick around another day or so."

"Well, eh . . . certainly," Barton spoke up. "But we don't want to be a burden."

"Absolutely no burden. I know those mountains above the springs better than anyone in the Territory. I'd like to point Cloverdale and the boys in the right direction."

Nelson Barton set down his blue enameled coffee cup. "What about the C.V.L. men? When do you expect them to return?"

"If Jedel is in Santa Fe, like they say, it will be weeks. But even if he's not, I'm guessing they will come in here with a stack of legal papers and a sheriff to evict. It seems to be the way corporations work."

"What about the gunfight with the C.V.L. men earlier?"

"They got carried away because of my reputation. This Burlington, or whatever his name is, he'll try to do it legal. Then later on he'll send in his hired guns. Actually, I wish you'd stick around a couple weeks until they do show up. I'd appreciate your advice about the so-called land grant papers."

"We must get to Phoenix," Barton nodded, "but there's no reason we can't wait a little longer."

"I'd appreciate more rest before we start out," Cancino offered.

"I agree with Julie," Reed said smiling. "Maybe we can wash out some of the road dust from these clothes. You do have a washboard and soap, don't you, Stuart?"

He glanced down at his clothing, then back at the women.

"Eh, yes, ma'am—although it might seem difficult to believe."

"Nelson, help me assist Julie to that big chair by the fireplace. Now, Stuart, you sit in here with Miss Cancino and visit while we straighten up."

Tucking a pillow behind her friend's back, Harriet Reed whispered, "It's your turn, girl!"

"Are you serious?"

"Go for it."

Even though the temperature hardly warranted it, Brannon stirred up the fire and added a couple of sticks of firewood.

"Julie, you're a tough girl. That was a bad bullet you took up in Prescott."

"Aren't they all bad?"

"What I meant was . . . sometimes a bullet doesn't do as much damage as other times. Anyway, what I'm trying to say is that I admire your courage—and your smile."

"My smile?"

"You've got one of the most beautiful, natural smiles in the world. Makes a man feel right at ease with you from the beginning."

"Thank you, Mr., I mean, Stuart."

He walked over to the mantle and lifted up a photograph that had been lying face down. "Did I show you my Lisa? Now, look at that smile. It's almost the same, don't you think?"

"I think," she said softly, "that if I have to compete with a woman that beautiful, I'll never have a chance."

"Julie, how old are you?"

"How old do you think I am?"

"That's one way to avoid an answer. You look about . . . twenty-three or twenty-four. But you're younger, right?"

"I'm nineteen."

"How old do you think I am?"

"Well, with all the things you've done . . . now don't get sore if I'm wrong . . . about forty?"

"You're a bit wide of the mark. But I'm going to be spending the rest of my life looking back. Do you know what I mean?"

"Not really."

"I'll always be talking about how things used to be, what I've done in the past, and about my Lisa. You don't want to live in my past. It's too violent, and too sad. Anyway, I'm not very good at expressing myself. What I'm saying is, if I was nineteen and we both had good legs, you'd have to run all the way to San Diego to keep me from catching you."

"You mean that? You're not just saying that?"

"I don't lie."

"No, I don't suppose you do. Stuart, would you say we are good friends?"

"We are new friends . . . yep, I would say good friends. I don't go around kissing total strangers on the lips, you know."

"Would it be all right if I told people down in Phoenix that I was a good friend of Stuart Brannon?"

"You certainly may do it, but I'm really not sure that will impress many folks." He laughed.

"It impresses me."

"Julie, you take it easy with that smile. You'll break a lot of hearts with that weapon."

"You know, Mr. Brannon, you have a very nice way of telling a girl you're not interested in her. I don't feel nearly as bad as I thought I would."

"I still owe you a dance."

"And I intend to make you pay. Can I give you some advice, Mr. Brannon?"

"Please do."

"You aren't going to find any woman on earth better than Harriet. I suppose you know that, don't you?"

"Yeah. I do."

"I just leave the two of you in here for a few minutes and Julie already has you saying, 'I do,'" Harriet Reed teased as she entered the room.

"Well, I do . . . need to get some rest. Harriet, could you help me?" Miss Cancino asked.

It was after dark, and Brannon was perched under a lantern on the front porch of the house when the soldiers all turned in. Harriet Reed came out of the house.

"Well, cowboy," she grinned, "are we going meet out on the porch again?"

"It's our destiny, Calypso."

"Did you sail by the siren without altering your course?"

"Yes, but I have to admit I tugged at the ropes that held me to the mast."

"When did you first read *The Odyssey?*"

"In a country schoolhouse in the middle of Texas when I was ten. And you?"

"In a New England boarding school when I was twelve. Some stories last a long time. That's the kind that I want to write."

"I believe you will. Now tell me something, Harriet, why did you push me and Julie into the living room together tonight?"

"Because you'd never get around to talking to her if I didn't."

"How did you know what I would say?"

"Intuition."

"Well, do you know what I'm going to say to you?"

"I suppose you want to tell me that you're madly in love with me, can't stand the thought of living without me, plead with me to marry you by Saturday, and insist on a honeymoon in the Sandwich Islands."

"What?"

"Well, maybe I was off a little. Oh, yes, Mr. Brannon, I really do know what you're going to say to me. But do you know what I am going to say to you?"

"I'd rather not guess."

"OK, Mr. Stuart Brannon, I'll give it to you straight. I like being around you. Somehow you're able to combine morality and integrity with a western recklessness that puts you in the middle of every major conflict within three hundred miles. I've spent my life hiding from all that, and it's been a boring life.

"The problem with you, Brannon, is that every woman has to compete with Saint Lisa who will never again ever have to raise her voice, say something dumb, comb her hair, or have female problems. Now before you get mad and throw me out on my ear, let me add, your love for your wife is part of your strength. If you felt any other way, I, for one, would be disappointed.

"But . . . here's what you didn't know. I think I can share you with her. In fact, I believe in time, you will be able to share some of your heart with me too. What I'm saying, Stuart Brannon, is that I'm not pushy, but I am persistent. Don't expect to excuse me with some wise and witty saying. I'm going to stick to you like mud to a hog."

"Mud to a hog? Is this Miss Harriet Reed talking?"

"Actually," she said with a laugh, "it was Katie McGregor."

"Who?"

"She's the heroine in my novel."

"She sounds like my kind of gal. I'd like to meet her sometime."

"Oh, you will, Mr. Brannon, I'm sure you will. Now it's your turn. What did you want to say to me?"

For the next several hours he told her.

So, dearest, with Mr. Brannon and the soldiers gone, I have time to write to you after all. I truly wish you could meet Julie. She's just like you—if you take away eight years at boarding school. I can't believe I was so insufferable toward her at first!

Well, after that conversation last night with Stuart, I feel that our relationship has made great progress. His normal reaction is to cut off all relationships with women as soon as he recognizes some attraction. This is one woman who won't let him do that. Anyway, don't go buying a wedding present real soon, but the day will come, girl—the day will come!

Give my best to Rachel.

Affectionately yours,
Miss Harriet Reed

"Some riders coming down, Harriet!"

She glanced over at Julie who pointed to the south road.

"Mr. Harvey?" she called across at the barn. "Is Mr. Barton over there?"

"Yes, ma'am."

"Tell him we have company coming in."

The whole party left at the ranch were standing on the front porch by the time the man and woman on horseback rode into the yard.

"Good mornin'," the woman called. "Is Stuart around?"

"He left on a little jaunt with the soldiers. May we help you?" Mr. Barton offered. "Say, aren't you Judge Quilici?"

"And you're Barton from the Land Office? My word, what are all you folks doing down here?"

"House guests, but our host slipped out with the troops."

"We noticed the tents. Is there Indian trouble?"

"Not yet," Barton replied. "Just a little scouting, I believe."

"Well, our ranch is just over a couple mountains from here, so we rode in to see how that injured foot of Stuart's is progressing."

"Uh-hum," Harriet Reed coughed.

"Oh, excuse me," Barton apologized. "Judge Quilici, may I introduce my wife, Gwendolyn, my sister-in-law, Miss Harriet Reed, and Miss Julie Cancino of Prescott. I believe you might have met Mr. Gonzales and Mr. Harvey from the Land Office."

"And," Judge Quilici added, "this is my wife, Sage."

"Sage?" Reed questioned. "S-a-g-e? How delightful. May I borrow it for a character in my novel?"

"A woman of high culture and beauty, no doubt," Mrs. Quilici teased.

"Listen," Harriet added, "you really must plan on staying the night. It will be late before Stuart returns, and I know he would want to visit with you."

Judge and Mrs. Quilici dismounted, and Mr. Harvey led their horses to the barn.

"Just how long have you known Stuart Brannon?" Sage asked.

"Oh, just since last fall. We first met him up in Colorado."

"Actually, Judge," Mr. Barton added, "I would appreciate your perspective on this Spanish land grant thing. These fellows that Brannon came up against. What legal authority do they have?"

The two men wandered back into the living room where they

spent most of the rest of the day pouring over papers that Barton had brought in his valise.

It was about one o'clock when Harriet returned to the porch and plopped down next to Julie who was reading a book.

"How do you pronounce this name?" she asked.

"Aga-mem-non," Harriet replied. "Julie, don't you think this is rather bizarre for all these people to be together on this ranch? It's like something historic is about to take place."

"Harriet, you've been reading too many books," she remarked. "Do you know what? I think I just wiggled my toes!"

"Seriously?"

"There's nothin' too serious about wiggling a toe. Unlace my right shoe, would you?"

Harriet tugged at the shoe and sock. Then, with foot lifted on a cushion, Julie wiggled her big toe.

"Did you see that! I did that!"

"You certainly did!"

"I never thought I'd be so happy wiggling my toe!"

Suddenly both women nearly doubled over in laughter. They noticed neither the dust nor the rattle of a wagon until the young man, with horse trailing behind, rolled a supply wagon into the yard. They turned to stare at the man, but they couldn't stop laughing.

"Where's Mr. Brannon? Who are you?" the young man called.

"And who are you?" Julie snickered.

"I'm Earl Howland, and I work for Mr. Brannon. Where is he? What are you doing here? Why are those tents out there? Whose horses are in the corral? And what's so funny?"

Reed caught her breath. "Excuse us, Mr. Howland. Believe me, we weren't laughing at you. We were laughing at Julie's toe. She can wiggle it! Look!"

"Who are you and why are you here?" Howland slowly bent over and lifted his rifle from the floor of the buckboard.

Sage Quilici came to the doorway.

"Earl! Glad you made it back safe."

"Mrs. Quilici, what's going on here?"

"Well, why don't you come on in and grab a little left-over dinner. These are all friends of Brannon's from Prescott. Come on and eat; then I'll fill you in. You can unload the wagon later."

Howland banged his dusty brown hat on the wagon, replaced it on his head, and climbed down.

"Earl Howland, I'd like you to meet Harriet Reed and Julie Cancino."

The women smiled.

"And this," Harriet giggled, "is Julie's famous wiggling toe!"

"Harriet! Really!" Julie blushed and smiled at Howland.

"You're the woman who got shot up in Prescott!" He nodded at Miss Cancino.

"How did you know?"

"Mr. Brannon said you had a smile that would melt the stiffness out of a boiled shirt."

"He did?"

"He's right, too. Nice to meet you, Miss Julie . . . and you too, Miss, eh, ma'am." He nodded at Harriet Reed. Then he followed Mrs. Quilici to the kitchen.

Harriet glanced at Julie.

"Didn't I say this was a historic day?"

"Miss Reed, just how old would you say Mr. Howland is?"

"I don't know, Miss Impressive Smile, but that young man is handsome enough to make more than your toes wiggle!"

"You know," Julie said with a grin, "I'm still a little hungry. Do you suppose you could help me into the kitchen?"

The Triple B had just settled down after Howland returned and unloaded supplies when another cloud of dust appeared coming down the road from the north.

Harriet motioned to Julie. "If we get two more visitors, we will qualify for our own post office."

"Well, as long as they're handsome men, I suppose we can find room." She shaded her eyes to peer at the tall rider with a thin mustache who rode straight up in the saddle.

The stranger tipped his hat. "I beg your pardon, ladies, I say

. . . is this the Brannon ranch, or did I get myself horribly lost again?"

"Mr. Fletcher?" Harriet questioned.

"Eh . . . Miss Reed? I do believe it's Miss Reed. It is still Miss Reed? My word, Brannon didn't get married yet, did he?"

"It's still Miss Reed. Stuart mentioned you were coming in sometime in the next few weeks. I don't believe he was expecting you so soon."

"Where is Brannon, and what exactly is going on here?"

"Well, if you'd like to put your horse with the others in the corral, I'll tell you."

It was one of those evenings when the sun stayed up forever, the breeze was mild, and every problem in the world seemed less severe. The whole crew sat out on the porch and in the yard after supper, getting acquainted and waiting for their host to return. About 9:00 P.M. most decided that Brannon and the troops would not ride in before morning, so they found their way to their quarters. Howland and Fletcher crowded into the bunkhouse with the other men.

Harriet Reed sat outside for a long while and then finally carried the lantern into the house.

"Did he come in yet?" Cancino asked from under the covers.

"No, but I'm sure he's safe, being with the troops."

"Or they're safe being with Brannon. I have a feeling that anyone married to him will spend many a night out on the porch worried sick."

"Yes, you're right about that."

"What do you think of the Englishman?"

Reed faked an English accent. "Mr. Fletcher? I say . . . he's quite an interesting chap." She turned off the lantern and crawled under the comforter.

"Are you wiggling those toes again!" She tried to sound serious.

Somewhere in the midst of more giggles, both fell asleep.

Deep in the middle of the night Reed thought she heard the troops ride in. She wanted to get up and check . . . but she was too sleepy.

Even Stuart Brannon couldn't wake me up now.

EIGHT

First came the sound of gunfire from the bunkhouse. Then a shout. Nelson Barton banged at their door. "Ladies, get dressed. There's trouble out front!"

"What is it?" Reed called.

There was no reply.

Harriet Reed cautiously pulled open the wooden shutter on the window and peeked out. The view that greeted her was a tranquil scene of a mountain slope to the east and the morning sun just cresting the ridge. Facing the back of the house, the small bedroom she shared with Miss Cancino offered no sight of the front yard and the roads leading out of the valley.

She helped Julie dress.

"No time to look beautiful, girl!"

"But what kind of trouble? Indian trouble?"

"I just don't know . . . put your arm around my neck."

"Harriet, I'm scared."

"Me too."

"I wish Mr. Brannon were here."

"Don't we all?"

"Is there an extra gun around?"

"A gun?" Reed questioned.

"It's the best way to meet trouble."

"Miss Cancino, you surprise me!"

"Harriet, I've spent my life livin' on the other side of town from folks like you."

"I did see a revolver hanging by the back door. Is that what you mean?"

"Yeah, I want it!"

Reed carried Julie Cancino, with revolver in hand, to the living room. They heard a clamor on the front porch.

Judge and Sage Quilici and Nelson and Gwendolyn Barton stood just outside the open front door. Two men were on horseback, and a third stood only a few feet from the Bartons.

"I know that man!" Cancino whispered.

"Who is he?"

"He beat up Sylvia one time—real bad."

The man threatened, "Look, Mister, I don't care who you are or how many women and kids you have in there. You're trespassing on private property."

"This is insane!" Barton shouted. "This Territory will not be run by two-bit criminals!"

With jarring quickness, the man's fist caught Barton on the chin and sent the land agent sprawling back against the door. Mrs. Barton cried out and stooped to assist her husband.

With her right arm clutching Harriet Reed's neck, Julie Cancino struggled to the doorway. Just as the man reached down for the revolver on his hip, Cancino shouted, "Mister, you touch that gun and you'll have a hole in your head big enough to drive a mule through!" She raised the cocked pistol within three feet of the man.

"That's a dangerous toy for a woman to be playing with! Surely you don't think I'm afraid of being shot by some saloon girl?"

"Surely you don't think some saloon girl would hesitate to separate what little brain you have from the rest of your worthless body!"

"Julie," Harriet whispered under her breath, "I think I'm going to faint!"

Speaking between clenched teeth, Cancino replied, "Don't you dare!"

"Well, boys," the man said to the riders without looking back at them, "I guess we'll just have to shoot our way out of here."

"I say now, I do believe you're correct about that!"

Everyone on the porch whipped about to see Fletcher, Howland, and Harvey all holding rifles. The other two covered the men on horseback, and Fletcher stepped up to the porch.

"Sorry we're late. We were trying to determine if the others were going to open fire."

"How many others?" the judge asked.

"Around fifty, I guess. Gonzales is keeping watch."

"So they brought a whole outlaw army!" Sage Quilici asserted.

"One shot from down here and they ride in, bullets flying. If you value these ladies' lives . . ." The man slowly reached for his gun.

Fletcher's rifle butt caught the man in the stomach; then the barrel crashed against his head. He tumbled off the porch and into the yard.

"Mr. Fletcher!" Reed gasped.

The two on horseback started to go for their guns, but rifles quickly pressed into their backs.

"My word! I've been around Brannon much too long! Judge, help me throw this old boy across his saddle," Fletcher called.

Then turning to Howland, he barked, "Pull their guns, bullets, and rifles."

"You cain't—" one started to complain. But the feel of a rifle barrel sliding up his back to his neck silenced him.

"These guns are being confiscated as evidence of assault and attempted extortion," the judge explained. "Since you are working for Warren G. Burlingame, we'll hold this proof until he shows up to claim them."

"When we come back, there won't be any evidence left," one man threatened.

"You are facing a judge, a presidential-appointed land agent, U.S. federal troops, assorted other guns, mean women, and Stuart Brannon. Is C.V.L paying you good enough for that? Before you boys come riding in here, I'd demand a raise," Fletcher roared.

"I don't see no troops!"

"You see those army tents, don't you? We aren't growing tomatoes in them!"

"If you go towards the buildings, we will have to ask the troops for assistance."

"You got no legal right to be here."

The judge waved his finger at the men. "Until any land grant is settled, this land belongs to Stuart Brannon."

"That's not what the attorneys say."

"Well," the judge continued, "you send down the lawyers, and we'll discuss the legalities of the matter. But anyone else who rides down here with gun drawn, threatening ladies, will be shot on sight."

"Hank Jedel's going to be mad—real mad. You don't think we'll just ride away, do you?"

"And you don't think we'll disappear, do you?" Sage Quilici offered.

"Well, it looks like a standoff."

"You can stand anywhere you want as long as it's not on the Triple B Ranch," Howland added.

"Earl, I never thought you'd double-cross us like this!"

Howland raised his rifle.

"Don't shoot him, Mr. Howland!" Cancino called.

He lowered the rifle.

"A man is known by his friends," Howland growled. "I make my stand with these folks. And you're making your stand with the likes of Jedel." He slapped the rump of the horse, and suddenly all three horses bolted back up the trail. At the top of the southern hill, the other riders were waiting.

"Mr. Barton, how's the jaw?"

"No damage . . . yet."

"Sorry about holding off, but we thought for sure the others would ride in. I think the tents fooled them."

Harriet began to breathe again. "It won't fool them for long."

"If Brannon and the others ride back soon, we should be all right."

"Will they really attack?" Reed asked.

"That's a good question. We'll need a quick defense," Fletcher replied. "My word, Brannon, I do wish you'd get home!"

Within fifteen minutes the six men and four women secured the bunkhouse, barn, and house. Harriet scurried to deliver breakfast to everyone.

"You look like Florence Nightingale moving through the troops in the Crimea," Fletcher remarked.

"And this . . . looks like a war!"

Stuart Brannon had every intention of riding to the upper end of the ranch and returning home the same day. But what they found in the mud near Jinete Springs caused him to reconsider.

"What do you think, Brannon . . . maybe a dozen ponies?"

Unable to dismount and remount, Brannon studied the tracks as he leaned over the saddle.

"Sergeant, it looks about that way. Of course, I've seen two Apaches make tracks look like a hundred, and I've seen fifty braves cover up their trail until you'd swear not even a jackrabbit had passed through."

"So what are you sayin'?"

"That a dozen is a good guess, but be prepared."

"You do agree that they're fresh?"

"Some of them still have water standing in them, and the grass is bent—with a warm, dry day like yesterday, I'd say last night or this morning. You going to follow them?"

"For a while. I need to find out how many there are. My orders were to apprehend Two Slash for questioning, push any others back onto the reservation, and locate an eastern trail through these mountains."

"Well, even if there's only a dozen or so, it will be difficult to get them out of these mountains."

"Is it all rocks and trees from here on up?"

"All except the caves and canyons."

"Well, I suppose we should return to the ranch, pack up camp, and then come back. But with these tracks so fresh, maybe we ought to follow them into the mountains for the rest of the day and try to determine just how many there are. That way we'll know whether to pursue or send for additional troops."

"Sounds reasonable." Brannon lifted his bad foot with his

hands and repositioned it. "Look, Sergeant, you'll need to stick to the tree line and contour around this mountain. There's no trail, but the boulders are too rough down below, and the timber is too thick up above. When you come to a long, steep draw with a little stream, you'll need to turn north and ride right up the stream. Then you'll—"

"Brannon, any chance I could talk you into riding on up there with us?"

"You know, with all those folks back at the ranch and—"

"They ain't going to leave until we return, right?"

"No, I don't suppose so."

"How about us ridin' up there until dark, makin' a little cold camp, and then return to the ranch tomorrow? If we get far enough away from the springs, maybe the tracks will be easier to read."

Brannon hesitated.

"Let's water the horses and grab a bite to eat. And I'll think on it, Sergeant."

Jenner helped Brannon ease down and then took care of El Viento. Brannon hopped over to some shade and propped his swollen foot up on a rock. Most of what he could see of the foot was purple and yellow.

Lord, when are the fights not my fights? Yet how can I send them up there? Just the sergeant and a bunch of kids. They don't know their way around these mountains yet. If I knew for sure there would be no fighting, I could let them wander around . . . but if they run into a band like Two Slash's, it would be a mighty rough battle. It's just that there's no one else around who could scout them through . . . Lord, what am I doing up here in the first place? I ought to be back at the house . . . yet if these boys get in a fight . . .

The sergeant walked over and sat down next to Brannon. "Well, Brannon . . . you going to ride with us?"

"With no boot and a foot the size of a head of cabbage I can't do you a whole lot of good. Still, if you get lost, I'll just have to come back up here and find you . . . so I guess I'll ride with you and save myself a trip. Now, mind you, I will be turning back at the crack of dawn."

"Sounds fair enough. You ready to go on?"

"Let's do it. This foot will either get better or fall off. Either way it will be an improvement!"

The Apaches stuck to the timberline, just as Brannon predicted, but they kept the horses more on the edge of the rock. That meant it was easy to follow their tracks but almost impossible to predict their number.

For three hours the soldiers rode single file with Brannon at the lead through the mountains. Each man's rifle lay across his lap, and his eyes scanned both the trees and the boulders.

Brannon halted the troops as they crossed a very small stream.

"Twelve horses, tops . . . maybe only ten," he told the sergeant.

"Could be Two Slash then?"

"Could be. Providing they stole more horses. We only left them with six, remember?"

"How far ahead of us?"

"I don't know. Sometime today."

"Do you think they know we're up here?"

"We'll find out."

"Well, that's what I came up here for. I believe we'll just camp here at the stream."

"If you're going to camp, it might be best to find a more defensible position."

"Do you think they might attack?"

"Nope. But up here you only get to be wrong once."

"Maybe we should go up into those rocks then?"

"Perhaps. Why don't you and the boys fill up the canteens, and Jenner and I will scout up there for a campsite."

Within a few minutes Brannon and Jenner were out of sight of the others.

"Mr. Brannon, how close do you figure we are?"

"To the Indians?"

"Yeah."

"Just a few miles, I suppose."

"Why don't we hurry up the trail and catch them?"

"What's the first rule I told you yesterday?"

"Eh . . . try to avoid a fight if you can?"

"Especially if they know you're coming," Brannon added. "My advice would be for you to never get too close, but just sort of herd them back onto the reservation. Then you can single out the troublemakers and deal with them one at a time."

"Makes sense to me."

It was a split-second, chilling stillness rolling down Brannon's back that caused him to rein up on El Viento. Jenner kept going, pulling slightly ahead of him.

He wanted to halt Jenner and listen.

He never got that chance.

It was a sickening thud.

Brannon didn't need to look. He had his rifle at his shoulder and had fired two shots before Jenner, with arrow in his chest, fell to the rocks. Brannon leaped out of the saddle, staggered, and fell to the ground. Jenner struggled to get his breath as Brannon fought to remove the arrow.

El Viento, followed by Jenner's horse, retreated back towards the creek. Brannon shielded Jenner and searched the rocks. He thought he saw movement on up the mountain to the right. Glancing at Jenner, Brannon leaned over and closed the eyelids over frightened, lifeless eyes.

Lord . . .

There was nothing Brannon could think of to say.

Knowing that the sergeant and the others would soon be coming up behind him, Brannon dragged himself through the rocks in pursuit of the Indian.

Maybe it's a trap to draw me into an ambush. If so, then they don't know about the sergeant and the other men. Maybe there's only a couple . . .

Stumbling, falling, mostly crawling, Brannon kept low behind the rocks and boulders as he inched his way up the mountain. Several tries at putting a little weight on his injured foot did little good. He resorted to just crawling along, dragging his right leg. After a few minutes of making little progress, Brannon dragged himself into the protection of the underside of a large boulder and glanced back down the mountain. From there he could see Jenner's body. Cloverdale and the others had spread out and were cautiously approaching their comrade on foot.

Then there was a slight grinding sound.

Like sandpaper across a rough surface.

Brannon knew the sound.

Moccasin on granite! He's above me. If I could only move quickly. He'll shoot Cloverdale . . . but I can't reveal my position . . . or can I?

Suddenly Brannon let out a blood-curdling war cry. Down below, Cloverdale and the others dove behind rocks with guns pointed toward Brannon.

At the same instant the warrior above him on the rock leaped down, throwing a knife at Brannon as he jumped. Brannon rolled away from the rock without time to pull a trigger. The Indian was on him before Brannon could raise the rifle.

In the duel for possession, the Indian's knee slammed down on Brannon's injured foot. For a split second he thought he was going to pass out, but with a final burst of strength he smashed the rifle barrel against the Indian's head.

It was only then that Brannon noticed the deep scars on the Indian's upper arms.

With head bleeding, the Indian scooped up his knife and charged at Brannon, who still lay on his back.

He pointed the rifle at the Indian, but the warrior was too quick.

The ill-aimed shot hit Two Slash in the shoulder and spun him completely around. He still faced Brannon. With left arm dangling, he again dove at Brannon.

The second shot ended his pursuit.

For a brief moment it was quiet.

"Brannon!" Cloverdale shouted.

He waved the barrel of his rifle at the troops. "Up here!"

"How many are there?"

"Don't know . . ." Brannon was so out of breath he could hardly shout.

"Can we send a couple men up to you?"

"No! Hold your positions. Watch the horses and dig in. They could come from any direction!"

"Is it Two Slash?"

"Yeah. He killed Jenner, but I took care of that."

"He's dead?"

Brannon looked again at the Indian's body.

"Yeah, he's dead."

It was a good fifteen minutes later when Cloverdale called, "Brannon, I'm coming up!"

"Keep low, Sergeant—real low."

Brannon wrapped his bandanna around his bleeding injured foot.

Cloverdale inched his way up, took a look at Two Slash, and then stared at Brannon's foot.

"Are you all right?"

"Oh . . . it got smashed and the pain's next to unbearable. But no new injuries."

"How'd it happen?"

"Jenner? Just like it always happens. We were riding out of those trees, and an arrow came out of nowhere. You never see them coming."

"The boys are pretty hot. They want to pursue."

"They want to chase them through these rocks at night?"

"No, I don't think so."

"Well, the way I got it figured—either they'll attack us before dark, or they'll retreat and ride all night. They could be back on the upper end of the reservation before dawn, and there's no way we could identify any of them."

"That might be, but my men aren't going to just ride away. They have to try to follow."

"Yeah . . . I know. How about we creep up this hill at least until the sun goes down. Then if we haven't found them, we head back down."

"In the dark?"

"Until we get to Jinete Springs. If they reach the reservation, you might as well wire the agent and let him handle it from there."

"You think it's safe to mount up?"

"I hope so, Sergeant. I really hope so."

After the horses were brought, several of the men tied Jenner's body to his saddle. Two of them approached the dead Apache with their knives drawn.

Brannon cocked his rifle and shouted at the men, "Don't touch him!"

"Are you going to scalp him, Mr. Brannon?"

"No one is going to scalp him!"

"But he killed Jenner!"

"And he's dead. You mutilate his body, and there will be twenty-five more warriors on the trail. Only next time you might not be around, and they'll ride right down Sunrise Creek to the Triple B."

"What are you going to do with him?"

"Throw him across the front of my saddle!"

Within moments the troops started climbing the rocky hillside. Progress was slow, and the sun had just slipped behind the western horizon when they came to the mouth of a shallow cave among the boulders.

"This was their camp!" Cloverdale called.

"Look, Sergeant, they lit out in a hurry toward the southeast."

"Straight for the reservation?"

Brannon rubbed his leg, which hurt too much to keep in the stirrup. "That's my opinion."

"Are we going to pursue?" one of the soldiers asked the sergeant.

Everyone, including Brannon, looked at Cloverdale.

"Nope."

"Sergeant!" one of the men yelled. "We found this pony over here!" He led a short gray horse over to Brannon and Cloverdale.

"Was he tied up or running loose?"

"Eh . . . tied. Why?"

"That means they left this pony on purpose."

"Why?"

"Because it belongs to Two Slash."

"So he could escape?"

"Nope. So we could send the body home."

"You going to send him home on that pony?" the man protested.

"Yep."

"Sergeant?" the soldier complained.

"The purpose is to stop the killin', not increase it," the sergeant barked. "Send it back to 'em like Brannon said."

They stumbled their way back down the mountain. The moon was full when they reached the creek. Brannon figured the night was half gone when, cold and tired, they reached the springs on the upper end of the Triple B Ranch.

They didn't make much of a camp.

They didn't need one.

The pain in Brannon's foot kept him awake most of the night. That and thoughts of Private Jenner.

Lord, why did I ask Jenner to go with me up in those rocks? Why did the arrow hit him and not me? Why did I stop and he go on? Why didn't I just ride back to the ranch this afternoon and let the troops go on their own? They might have gotten lost and never stumbled into those Apaches at all.

Both sides fightin' for what they think is right. But only one side will win. Maybe . . . maybe it will never be resolved. A violent land ruled by violent men? It'll be different someday—if there's anyone left alive to enjoy it.

I am not a violent man!

Cloverdale didn't push his troops the next morning, but most of the men awoke by sun-up. The talk around the campfire centered on things like saddles, weather, and food. No one really wanted to say anything. Several of the men came over to Brannon.

"Did ya have to fight him hand to hand, Mr. Brannon?"

"He jumped me before I could get my rifle up."

"How come you screamed like that? It just about turned my hair gray."

"I was afraid he would shoot one of you. He didn't know I was that close; I was hoping to startle him into making a mistake."

"I guess it worked."

"Yeah." Brannon sighed. "It worked this time."

The grass was just as tall, the flowers just as pretty, and the water that trickled down Sunrise Creek was just as cold as when they had ridden up the trail the day before. But the mood of the troops differed.

They want a fight.

They're angry and afraid.

They want vengeance.

It's got to be justice, Lord. This country has got to be settled on justice, not revenge!

Sergeant Cloverdale spurred on up beside Brannon.

"Think we'll ride on down to Phoenix with Barton. I'll need to know if this is part of a wider outbreak or just one band."

"I'm sure the folks will like the protection."

"I don't know . . ." Cloverdale paused. "I figure some of them ladies were just as happy to stay right on the ranch."

"You ever think about quitting the army, Sergeant?"

"Every time I lose a Jenner . . . or a Taylor. I must have quit in my mind a hundred times."

"But you never do?"

"Brannon, this is all I know."

"Oh, that sounds good to the recruits, but it doesn't wash with me. I've run across ex-soldiers panning for gold, breaking wild horses, running saloons, punching cattle . . . you name it."

"Well . . . maybe so, Brannon. Maybe so. Why do you keep at it? You don't have to be up here. Me and Jenner didn't have a choice once we signed on. So why don't you pull out of this country?"

"I have too much invested in it. Not just time and money, but heartaches, sorrows, and delights as well."

"There's a high cost to settle a new land," the sergeant observed.

"Yep, it takes a Jenner and a Taylor, a Lisa and the baby, a young Julie and a stray bullet . . ."

"And a Stuart Brannon?"

"Yeah . . . a Stuart Brannon and a Sergeant Cloverdale. But we're just too close to the finish line to quit now. The cost has been great, and I guess I want to stick around long enough to make sure it was all worthwhile."

"Yeah, I guess that's it, isn't it, Brannon? Something keeps nagging at a man's insides . . . telling him it will all be worthwhile. Stuart, did you ever think of joining the army?"

"Never."

"Too bad."

"Sergeant!" one of the men called. "You want to look at this?"

They looked up to see a private who had been scoping the ranch, which was still a good distance away.

"What are you lookin' at?" Cloverdale asked.

"He was trying to spot Miss Julie!" another of the men teased.

"Eh, I was . . . just, you know—looking to see if everything is all right."

"And?"

"It looks like . . . it looks like there's, ah, a lot of men down there!"

"What? Where?" Brannon whipped around on El Viento and grabbed the brass telescope from the man's hand.

"What is it?" the sergeant asked.

"Collectors! Casa Verde Land Corporation Collectors!"

"How many?"

"Forty . . . fifty. I can't tell."

"And the Bartons? What about Miss Julie?" one of the soldiers asked.

"From where that gang is camped, high up on that south road, I'd say it's a draw," Brannon reported.

NINE

"Can these bones live?" Brannon mumbled.

"What?" Cloverdale asked.

"Ezekiel 37—the valley of dry bones. I left this ranch covered with the bones of dead cattle. Now the place is covered with people. Do you know there are more people on this piece of ground right now than have ever been on it before?"

"Not exactly a quiet, remote ranch at the moment. What do we do?"

"I won't ask government troops to settle my land claim, so you might want to stay out of the line of fire."

Cloverdale looked back at his men and then glanced down at the ranch house.

"We, of course, try to avoid getting entangled in domestic disputes. Those fall under the jurisdiction of the county sheriff. However, since we've just lost one of our men due to an unprovoked ambush by Indians, I've decided that we'll continue to camp at the Triple B Ranch to try to prevent future Indian attacks on settlers."

"And if you happen to be fired on while doing your duty?" Brannon asked.

"We will, of course, defend ourselves."

"Thanks, Sergeant."

"What do we do first?"

"I really don't think they'll fire on the U.S. Cavalry, but ride down with rifles ready. If it doesn't compromise your defense, I'd

like for us to ride in single file . . . stretching out the line as long
as we can. They'll have us outnumbered three to one, but those
odds aren't bad if we can make it to the yard."

"And if we don't?"

"Then you boys will have to do whatever army regulations
allow. I'm going on into the yard and defend my ranch."

"Line 'em up . . . spread them out . . . and take it slow," the
sergeant hollered.

Brannon led the column of troops right down the middle of the
valley toward the ranch house and barn. Cloverdale followed him;
then came Jenner's body and horse, then the other troops.

"Sergeant," Brannon called back, "have you got a bugler?"

"Yep. What do you want?"

"How about taps?"

"For Jenner?"

"Yeah . . . and to give the rest of them serious thought."

Fletcher and Howland were stationed in the bunkhouse, closest to the Collectors. Gonzales and Harvey guarded the horses and
the barn. The Bartons stood guard at the back door, Judge and
Mrs. Quilici at the front. Julie Cancino insisted on sitting on the
front porch in her chair with a revolver in each hand.

They all watched as the Collectors mounted up, swept out in a
wide arc, and paced slowly down the hill. Harriet Reed, acting as
runner, had just taken more ammunition out to Fletcher and
Howland in the bunkhouse. At Julie's insistence she wore a gun,
holster, and belt over her shoulder.

"What are they doing?" she asked.

"Moving in 'til they draw fire," Howland suggested.

"Then what?"

"Then they can say they were defending themselves."

"They really want to kill us?" she asked.

"They only want us to leave, but they'll stop at nothing to see
that happen!"

Suddenly she heard an eerie, distant sound.

"What's that?" she asked Fletcher.

"A horn, perhaps?"

"Where?"

Howland, Fletcher, and Reed stepped out the door to gaze around. Judge and Mrs. Quilici stood on the porch of the house.

"My word, it's taps!" Fletcher exclaimed.

"Look! Up the valley," Howland shouted.

"It's the troops!" Reed added, holding her hand over her eyes to try and spot the column.

"They're coming back!" she yelled across to Julie Cancino. "But why taps? You only play that at the end of the day."

"Or when someone dies," Howland added.

"Dead? Oh, no!" Reed panicked. "No! Not Brannon, no!"

Suddenly she darted towards the house.

"Really, Miss Reed—" Fletcher began.

But instead of running to the house, she skirted the south side of the building and began to run up the valley towards the oncoming troops. She hiked up her long white dress above her ankles and started to run faster.

Please, Lord, not Brannon. No! We need him! I need him! Please . . .

Just as she broke out into the open behind the house, a rider on a bay horse dashed out from the band of Collectors and circled the ranch.

"He's heading for Miss Reed!" Howland yelled.

Fletcher began to sprint after her, but a barrage of bullets forced everyone back into the buildings, except Miss Cancino. She absolutely refused to be budged from her chair.

For a few moments those in the barn, house, and bunkhouse returned fire. No one could see Harriet Reed at all. The distance between the warring parties was so great that all shots, from both sides, did little more than kick up dust.

Brannon saw the Collector break out and gallop towards the back of the house. Then dozens of shots rang out, like a string of distant firecrackers on the Fourth of July.

He spurred El Viento up a notch, and the soldiers did the same.

Suddenly, he saw her.

*It must be Miss Reed. Julie can't walk. Mrs. Barton wouldn't
. . . that's what he's after—Harriet!*

Brannon cocked the Winchester and spurred El Viento. The big
black horse sensed the urgency and bolted away from the troops
and down the valley.

She's too far. I can't get there! Harriet, go back!

Reed heard rifle fire and the rumble of hoofbeats. She stopped
to catch her breath. She looked up and was surprised to see how
far away the column of troops remained. A stinging slap of a
hemp rope banged against the back of her neck. She almost tumbled head over heels. Then, abruptly, she was yanked off her feet,
a rope around her waist. Dragged backwards in the dirt, Reed
grabbed for the revolver in the holster still clinging to her shoulder.

"I'll shoot!" she screamed.

The man with the dirty face on the bay horse stopped dragging
her for a moment to reach for his own gun. In sheer terror Harriet
pulled the trigger. Nothing happened but a feeble click.

"No!" she screamed.

"Took a shot at me, did ya?" he sneered. "Well, that makes it
self-defense, don't it?"

He aimed his revolver. In panic, Harriet pulled back the hammer and squeezed the trigger again. This time the Colt .45 blasted
away sending a bullet right behind the ear of the horse, which
staggered and fell backwards pinning the man's right leg as it fell.

"You killed my horse!" he screamed, trying to yank his leg free
and retrieve his weapon.

Harriet's entire body quaked. She couldn't close her mouth. She
tried to stand, the rope still cinched around her waist, but she collapsed to her knees.

"I'll kill you!" the man was ranting.

Suddenly, another horse rode up behind her. She whipped
around with the gun pointed and cocked. When she saw it was

Brannon, she dropped the gun, fell to her hands and knees, and started to sob.

She didn't want to cry. But she couldn't stop.

Brannon rode past Miss Reed and straight at the downed gunman.

"She killed my horse!" the man still screamed. Seeing Brannon, he found the strength to wrench his foot out from under the horse and roll over and grab his revolver.

Brannon dove from the saddle, and the barrel of the Winchester crashed alongside the man's ear just as his hand grabbed the handle of his revolver. A shot fired into the dirt, and the unconscious man crumpled.

Crawling around the dead horse, Brannon hurried to Reed. She swayed on her hands and knees, covered with dirt, in hysterics. He sat on the ground next to her and pulled her to himself, rocking her in his arms.

"It's OK, Harriet . . . it's all right now . . . everything's fine."

It was a long time before she stopped crying.

When she did, she and Brannon were surrounded by army troops, and the man who had chased her was gagged and tied.

"Sergeant," Brannon called, "could you help me to my saddle?"

Once aboard El Viento, he again addressed the sergeant. "Could you hand up Miss Reed? She can ride in with me."

Brannon cradled her on his lap, and she held her arms tight around his neck. Neither of them said a word.

The gunfire at the ranch had stopped as both sides watched the drama in the valley behind the house. The soldiers rode in first, followed by Cloverdale leading the bound Collector on foot, then Brannon and Reed.

The sergeant quickly stationed his men around the circumference of the yard and tied the prisoner to a tree.

Brannon rode up.

Julie Cancino was beside herself trying to stand.

"Brannon! Is Harriet—? Did she get hurt?"

"Judge! Sage?" Brannon exclaimed as he encountered the Quilicis. "What are you doing in all this?"

"Just a simple neighborly visit, Stuart." Mrs. Quilici assisted Harriet off the horse and immediately led her into the house. Gwendolyn Barton helped Miss Cancino, and all four women disappeared into the back rooms.

"Good heavens, Stuart, I'm gone for a few weeks and you start a war!"

Brannon whipped around in the saddle to see Edwin Fletcher sprinting up.

"Edwin! Well, it's about time you got here!" Brannon slipped out of the saddle and collapsed on his bad foot. He grabbed out for Fletcher and caught the Englishman around the neck.

"I say, Brannon, is that your foot or an eggplant?"

"Put me on that bench," Brannon ordered, "and then tell me what's going on here."

"Me? I was going to ask you the same thing!"

Brannon and Fletcher had barely begun to visit when Howland shouted from the bunkhouse, "A rider's coming, and he's waving a white flag!"

Everyone watched as a man on a paint horse trotted down towards the buildings. As he entered the yard, he held the reins high with both hands.

"Brannon," he shouted, "you and me need to talk!"

Earl Howland followed the man across the yard with his rifle held to the man's back. "Jedel, if there is any hint of deception in this visit, you will be shot dead on the spot."

"Yeah, and if I don't ride back up there unharmed, those boys will come crashing down that mountain shooting everyone in this place."

"OK," Brannon said with a shrug, "we've got the formalities taken care of. I presume you rode in here to apologize for your unsocial behavior."

"I rode in here," Jedel shouted, "to give you all one last warning. I want to make this clear. You are all trespassing on Casa Verde Land Corporation property, which is owned by Burlingame and Associates through a deeded Spanish land grant. This site has in fact been designated the headquarters, and, as such, we'll need you to clear the premises before nightfall."

"We've been through this with your other boys," Brannon reminded him.

"Yes. Well, I believe it's important for everyone to understand the gravity of the situation. Of course, those of you who happen to be caught here as guests will be allowed to leave, taking either the north or south roads. You will not be followed or harassed in any way."

"Just like Miss Reed wasn't harassed coming out to meet the troops?" Fletcher challenged.

"That was totally unauthorized, I assure you. Sergeant, since army troops are not supposed to be used to settle domestic disputes, I presume you will be leaving soon?"

"Jedel," Cloverdale roared, "I will leave whenever I want to! We're staying here to protect settlers from Indian attack."

"But there aren't any Indians around here."

"Mister, I've got to bury one of my best men who was bushwhacked up in those hills last night. So don't go telling me where Indians is or ain't."

"Then you aren't moving your troops?"

"Not until threat of Indian attack subsides or I'm ordered to leave."

"That can be arranged."

"Don't threaten me," Cloverdale barked.

"Then, do I understand that all of you are staying?"

"Every one of us," Nelson Barton replied.

"Well, it's a dumb choice. You might be chased out, carried out, or drug out—but none of you is staying in this valley."

The judge marched to the front. "That grant has not been approved by Congress. By what authority do you make such claims?"

"By the authority of fifty armed men!"

"Forty-nine," Brannon corrected and nodded toward the man tied and gagged at the tree.

"The fact of the matter is, this property will be secured for the Casa Verde Land Corporation. We will attempt to do that without injury to innocent bystanders, U.S. troops, or ladies. But if you insist upon staying in the line of fire, I can make no guarantees."

Brannon stood to his feet and staggered over to the man.

"Jedel, I'm surprised at your sudden conversion to bravery. The last we met up in Black Canyon, you were trying to bribe the sheriff into letting you go to Mexico. You were a worthless murderer then, and you've done nothing to show any improvement. The only one here that needs to make a decision is you."

With lightning speed Brannon pulled his pistol, cocked it, and laid the barrel up against Jedel's temple.

"Have you ever thought about what it is in life that's worth dying for, Jedel?"

"W—w—what?" he stammered.

"Look around at this ranch . . . you see, I've already decided that it's worth dying for. You and those men up there are going to have to come to the same conclusion!"

Then Brannon reset the hammer and hobbled back to the bench.

"What about all these others, Brannon?" Jedel screamed. "Do they want to die for your so-called ranch?"

"They're all free to go."

"And I certainly hope they do."

"It might be a long time," Judge Quilici warned.

"I don't think so, Judge," Jedel sneered.

"Jedel, you bore me," Brannon replied. "Get on your horse and get out of here. You have threatened the lives of honest men, soldiers, and some of the Territory's most charming women. I will not tolerate that on my ranch. If you ride up here again, I will personally throw you off."

"You're making a grievous mistake that could cost the lives of innocent bystanders! Their blood will be on your hands, Brannon!"

"And take that worthless hired man of yours with you. We're not about to spend a dime feeding him. We're keeping his rifle, handgun, and saddle to be sold and the money given to Miss Reed for the damage done to her dress and person. Is that a fair ruling, Your Honor?" he asked the judge.

"It would certainly be a minimum sentence," Quilici replied.

"You folks are all at the wrong place at the wrong time!" Jedel shouted. "This is a historic spot! This is where the DePalma-Revera Land Grant will be settled—not in Tucson or Washington, DC. And all of you are on the wrong side of the line!" Jedel threw his left foot into the stirrup, then pulled it back down, and turned. "Brannon, I should have killed you years ago. You're a marked man. There'll be another grave up by those piñons before long. You aren't riding out of this valley alive!"

"I'm not riding out of this valley at all."

Jedel mounted his horse and rode out by the bound man. Howland released him from the tree, still hand-tied and gagged.

Jedel forced the man to trail along after him as they worked their way back up to the others.

"He's right about one thing, Stuart," Judge Quilici intervened. "A little Arizona history is going to be made right here."

"Oh, yes, I can see the title of the novel," Fletcher droned, "*Brannon Blasts the Collectors!*"

"You folks will have to excuse our foreign cousin here." Brannon scowled. "His literary background makes him a tad dramatic!"

"Hah!" Fletcher shouted. "In the confusion, I forgot to give you this present I picked up at a bookstore in San Francisco!" He slapped a small book into Brannon's hands.

"What!" Brannon exclaimed. "Where did you get this? What is this?"

"As you can plainly see, it is *Brannon Tames the Town* by Mr. Hawthorne H. Miller. I rather like the lithograph on the cover . . . although Rose Creek looks slightly too European."

"But . . . he can't . . . I didn't authorize . . . this is—"

"Say, Mr. Brannon," Earl Howland spoke up, "can I read that book sometime?"

"It's a popular number in San Francisco, and I hear New York City is flocking to get a copy," Fletcher mused. "For fifty cents more I could have purchased a volume signed by Mr. Stuart Brannon himself. It was nice of you to sign all of those, Stuart."

"This is . . . this is . . ." Brannon stammered.

"This is the West, Stuart," Judge Quilici chided. "I do believe a dime novel is the least of your current problems."

Brannon tugged off his black hat and scratched the back of his head. "Well, let's set some kind of guard duty around here," he mumbled. "*Brannon Tames the Town!* I can't believe it!"

Within a few minutes Brannon had reset all the defenses.

"Sergeant, I don't want to use your men for this land squabble. But just having you camped out here will be a deterrent. So withdraw to that area around your tents, and do whatever you need to. We'll keep one man at the bunkhouse, one at the barn, and one here on the porch. If they make a move during the daylight, we'll have time to set up before they can get here. The others can rest up and take shifts."

"Do you think they'll actually attack?" Fletcher asked.

"They have to try something. Those men will get restless sitting on a hillside day after day. If they don't do something, they'll start to drift on out of here."

"Stuart Brannon is going to just sit around and wait for someone to start shooting? My word, are you growing old?"

"Somehow land disputes in this Territory have to be settled on a basis other than who has the most guns!"

I am not a violent man.

After surveying all the area, Brannon checked in with Sergeant Cloverdale.

"You're walking on that foot now?" the sergeant asked.

"Thanks to this crutch that Howland made for me. I think Two Slash busting it open again helped it heal faster. Drained it out, or something. Anyway, what's your current spyglass report?"

"Looks like they're settling down for a siege."

"Just a matter of who waits it out the longest?"

"At least, that's what they want us to believe. Jedel and two others rode out on the south road."

"Going to get further instructions, no doubt."

"Or reinforcements," the sergeant offered.

Brannon limped slowly back across the yard to the main house. He met Gwendolyn Barton in the living room.

"Ma'am," he asked, "how's Miss Harriet doing?"

"Why don't you go check? I believe she would like to see you."

Brannon hobbled down the hall and knocked on the door.

"Excuse me . . . may I come in?"

"Please do," Miss Cancino called out.

Reed reclined on the bed, and Julie Cancino sat in a chair next to her.

"Well, who is taking care of whom?" he asked.

"We're a pair, we are," Cancino said laughing.

"When it comes to gunfights, I'm afraid Julie has me beat. You know that was the first time I've ever fired a gun. I can't believe I shot the horse. What I mean is, I can't believe that I actually tried to shoot that horrible man!"

"You had to protect yourself. Why were you running out there anyway?"

"You know," Julie Cancino interrupted, "if you two need to talk alone, you could just shove me out into the hall or something."

"Are you trying to leave me in this room alone with Mr. Brannon?" Harriet chided. "You stay right where you are and wiggle those toes! Did you hear that she can wiggle her toes?"

"The movement is coming back?" Brannon exclaimed.

"Maybe." Cancino beamed.

Turning to Harriet Reed, Brannon said softly, "You didn't answer my question."

"I ran out there because I had a horrible, sinking feeling that they were playing 'Taps' for you. I panicked and now I'm horribly embarrassed."

"Nothing embarrassing about being scared."

"Well, what I'm most ashamed of is that I prayed that it would be anyone else but you. It was unchristian. I had little sympathy for the soldiers. I do hope the Lord will forgive me. It was inexcusably selfish."

Brannon stared at Reed for a moment.

"You know," he finally said, "I don't think I've ever seen you with dirt on your face before. It becomes you."

"Boy, that Brannon is a sweet-talkin' thing," Julie teased. "What he's saying is, 'Girl, wash that face!' If you two are finished, maybe we can get cleaned up a bit."

"Do you think they'll try anything, Stuart?"

"Not with Jedel gone."

"So we just wait it out?"

"Yep, both sides perched and ready for battle hoping that the other one backs out before any shots are fired."

He spent the next hour sitting on the bench in front of the house discussing the situation with Nelson Barton and Judge Quilici.

"As I understand it, absolutely no one has clear title to a land grant until the Congress says so."

Barton paced along the porch. "The Surveyor-General of the Territory has the responsibility of ascertaining the origin, nature, character, and extent of all claims to land under the laws, usages, and customs of Spain and Mexico. He submits his report to the Secretary of the Interior, who gives it to Congress for a vote. If it passes, they issue the party a patent deed on the land."

"So," the judge added, "there's a lot of politickin' in Washington about these grants."

"Which Burlingame and his gang are very good at," Brannon added.

"That's correct, but I'm convinced that this is a fraudulent claim."

"Which means the Surveyor-General will recommend turning it down?"

"Without question." Barton nodded.

"But if Burlingame can pull strings, he can at least keep it tied up in Congress for quite a while," the judge chimed in. "And that means continuing to extort rent money from lots of folks."

"If the Surveyor-General reports not only a false claim, but also a purposeful attempt at deception, that would cut Casa Verde Corporation's congressional support."

"Would that end the matter?" Brannon asked.

"For all practical purposes."

"So you've got to prove that Burlingame or his attorneys falsified documents, changed dates and names, forged signatures—or at least knowingly bought such documents from someone else who did those things."

"Which is all pert' near impossible to prove while sitting down here on the ranch," Brannon exclaimed. "What we need to do is all go down to Tucson and examine the documents."

"Yes, that's true."

"Or have the Surveyor-General bring all the papers here!" the judge offered.

"Would he do that?"

"At the request of Mr. Barton and myself, he might."

"I believe the judge is right. On-site verification would be a part of his report. It might be worth a try. But how do we inform him?"

Brannon glanced at Quilici. "Judge, I have a big favor to ask of you and Sage."

"Oh?"

"I want the two of you to ride out of here. Tell the Collectors you need to get back to your ranch and then keep going. Go straight to Tucson and talk to the Surveyor-General to see if he will agree to come up here."

"It might take days . . . even weeks," Quilici warned.

"It's either that or settle it with guns. If we shoot it out, I will regret not having exhausted every other possibility."

"Do you think they'll let the judge ride out of here?" Barton asked.

"Yep, he's too important to shoot. Besides, if they think our resolve to stick around is weakening, they might just be content to sit still and not do anything for a while, hoping others will leave."

"I hate to cut down your defenses," the judge added.

"We'll manage. Will you do it?"

"Let me step into the kitchen and check with Sage."

Within thirty minutes Judge and Mrs. Quilici rode their horses up the trail to the south. Brannon stood with a spyglass in hand.

"Four men met them on the road," he called to the others. "They're talking . . . the judge is pointing towards the house. Sage said something . . . there! They left! They're on their way! Sergeant, watch to see if any of those Collectors try to follow them."

It was four tense days later before they observed Jedel ride over Despoblado Pass alone and reenter his camp. And for four days Brannon had noticed increasing anxiety build among those staying at his ranch.

At supper he called a meeting.

Julie was back sitting on the front porch, and Harriet was wearing a different dress.

"I think they'll try something tonight. The longer we keep possession of these buildings, the better our chances."

"Will they try to kill all of us?" Miss Cancino asked.

"I don't think they'll try to kill anyone other than me, and maybe Earl. They just want to scare the rest of you into leaving. If he got hold of Burlingame, I would expect some attempt to evict us that doesn't harm the ladies. If I were them, I'd try to burn us out."

Fletcher spoke up. "How will they get that close? Use a diversion?"

"I suppose."

"What will we do?"

"Extra guards—and water and wet blankets to put out a fire."

Howland scowled. "Is that all we can do?"

"Nope. We can set fire to their camp first."

"Wh—what?" Miss Reed gasped.

"Now that's the Brannon we know and love," Fletcher quipped.

"We'll need to do it in a nonviolent sort of way, of course." Brannon pulled out his revolver and spun the chamber. "As soon as I figure out one."

Handing him a plate of stew and a piece of bread, Miss Reed sat down next to him.

"You changed your dress," he commented.

"Mine are all filthy." She grimaced. "I borrowed this one from Julie."

"I noticed."

"What do you mean, Stuart Brannon, that you 'noticed'?"

"I noticed you don't seem to fill it out as well as Miss Cancino does."

Suddenly her elbow flew in Brannon's direction, and the entire contents of his plate dumped into his lap.

"Oh, my, I'm terribly sorry," she huffed. "Maybe Miss Cancino can assist you in cleaning up. I need to go to my room and slip into something that fits better!"

"Boy, Brannon, you're a real charmer!" Cancino laughed. "I'm sure glad I dumped you when I had the chance."

"Go wiggle your toes, Cancino." Brannon glared as he tried scraping the stew off his duckings with a spoon.

TEN

I think we're all set, Mr. Brannon." Earl Howland approached the barn where the others were standing.

Brannon pulled his revolver from his holster and slipped a bullet out of his belt and into the sixth chamber.

"We going to need a full load?" Howland asked.

"Perhaps. Cloverdale and men will come up and help put out any fires. But if it comes to a gun battle, they've got to defend themselves first. Now we've got to get our attack planned out."

"Actually, Stuart," Fletcher queried, "we aren't going to try to set fire to their camp, are we? I mean, there's nothing up there to burn."

"What I had in mind," Brannon explained, "was a response that would remind them that every attack on the ranch would cost them something."

"So what kind of response did you have in mind?" Fletcher questioned.

"I figure if they start trying to set a fire down here, we'll burn down their chuck wagon."

"What? I say, that doesn't sound horribly drastic considering what they will attempt!"

Brannon leaned against a hitching rail to take some weight off his injured foot. "Edwin, I'm trying real hard not to have any more killings. I don't want to give those Collectors any justification for riding in here, guns blazing. As for the chuck wagon . . ." He turned to Howland. "Earl, you've ridden with the wagon. What do you think?"

"You burn down the chuck and you just might start a war. Besides their supplies, that wagon will be filled with bedrolls, personal belongs, extra bullets—you name it. I've known whole crews to quit when the chuck wagon's lost."

Fletcher glanced across the yard at the flickering lights in the house. "Just how do you propose to do this pusillanimous deed?"

"Well, one of us will just crawl up there through the tall grass and wait until they start something. When they see their own rig burning, they might have second thoughts about pressing the attack."

"You really think that will catch their attention."

"Guaranteed. A couple sticks of dynamite are hard to ignore."

"Dynamite?"

"Yep. Earl brought me a boxful from Florence. I was planning on using it up near the springs to build a diversion pond. I believe I can spare a couple of sticks."

"How many of us will it take to go up and complete this counterassault?"

"One."

"Who?"

"Me."

"But you can hardly walk across the yard, even with a crutch!"

"Exactly. That makes me next to useless in carrying water and putting out fires. BUT . . . quite handy at crawling."

"I'll do it, Mr. Brannon," Howland volunteered.

"Thanks, Earl, but I need you here."

"What if they don't attack?"

"Then we wait until they do."

"You mean night after night?"

"Yep."

Within twenty minutes Brannon was giving final instructions before he left.

"Stuart, I say, are you able to pull this off?"

"We'll find out. In one hour turn off all the lanterns and mind your positions. I expect they won't make a move until about an hour after the lanterns are out."

"What do we do if there's no diversion?"

"Try not to let them burn down the place. If you have to let a building go, abandon the bunkhouse—then the barn. And don't let the women get hurt. If they burn us out . . . well, we'll fight them from the rocks."

"Mr. Brannon, where's your Winchester?"

"Can't carry it, Earl."

"Which way you heading out?"

"Through the back of the barn, up the hill towards the piñons, then over to their camp. Take your positions . . . and I'll meet you for breakfast."

"Why the back of the barn? It's a pretty dark night."

"Because I don't know how far down the hill they have men stationed."

Brannon hobbled his way through the barn, tossed the crutch into the corner, and dropped to his knees. Two sticks of dynamite were tucked into his left coat pocket. Caps, fuse, and matches were in the other. He had one Colt in his holster and another in his left hand. He kicked the bottom barn board loose, pried it away from the building, and crawled out. His black hat fell to the dirt, and he tossed it back inside the barn.

It wasn't exactly a crawl, but it certainly wasn't a walk. By dragging his right foot, Brannon scooted along in the dirt behind the corrals and across the rutted path that served as a road into the ranch. Stars cleared overhead. No sign of a moon. He got to the foot-high grass at the base of the hill and struck out diagonally towards the two piñon pines and the grave sites.

Nobody will be sitting at those graves on a dark night.

Lord, You know I've got to hold onto this ranch. I don't have it in me to let go. There's got to be a way . . . some way to do it without killing half the people on the place!

His right hand was nearly raw and his trousers covered with dirt by the time he reached the piñons and the graves. Even though the night was beginning to cool, sweat plowed through the dirt on

his face and neck. His right foot throbbed. So far, he had seen no
one and heard nothing.

Within a few minutes of his arrival, he saw the flickering
lanterns go out back down at the ranch. Immediately, all the
campfires of the Collectors were snuffed out as well. Brannon
crawled towards their camp.

He soon developed a pattern of dragging himself about five
feet, then stopping to listen for sounds of a night guard. He was
beginning to have doubts as to whether he had the strength to
crawl all the way back to the barn.

Hearing footsteps, he threw himself flat into the grass.

"Smiley?" a voice whispered about twenty feet to the left of
him.

"Yeah?" came a reply from in front of him.

"You're supposed to move over closer to camp. We'll be going
down in less than an hour. You seen anything?"

"Yeah, over by those graves."

"Did you check it out?"

"I ain't going over there. It was probably just a coyote."

"Yeah . . . the women are in the house; Howland and the
Englishman are in the bunk; Brannon and the other two are in the
barn."

How do they know that? They've been scoping us!

"I don't know how I got stuck drawing guard," one man complained.

"You can trade tomorrow night."

"You mean, you boys are goin' to leave something until tomorrow?"

"Yeah, they said we're aiming for the house tonight. Ain't even
going to try to torch the other buildings."

The house! Lord, protect the women!

"The boys should have the roads blocked by now. They even
sent six men around by the crick. They ain't going to run away
from this!"

"Is Jedel still jumpy?"

"You'd think it was Robert E. Lee himself down there. Brannon
can't be all that good."

"Don't tell that to Hank Jedel!"

If he had possessed two good legs, Brannon would have hurried down the hill to warn the others. The only thing he could do was act quickly on the chuck wagon and hope this would bring some of the attackers back to their own camp.

When the men moved on, he swung around the camp to the high side and then scooted down towards the campsite, searching the dark horizon for the profile of the chuck wagon. A slight outline against the starlit night gave him some direction. He moved quickly forward.

He was now not more than fifty feet from where their campfire had been earlier. The core of the camp was empty.

Maybe three guards, but all on the perimeter. A wrangler with the horses and a cook. The cook's around here somewhere!

Scooting flat on the ground, Brannon figured he was now within thirty feet of the chuck wagon.

I've got to get this dynamite into the wagon! If it bounces to the ground, it will make more noise than damage.

Suddenly, he heard footsteps coming near him. Without making a sound, Brannon pulled his revolver from the holster. He didn't dare click back the hammer. Whoever it was stepped only a few feet from his head and sneaked straight towards the chuck wagon.

Then he heard a rattling of pots and pans.

No! Don't start cooking now!

"Hey!" a voice shouted out from the other side of camp. "Who's gettin' in my wagon!"

The pots and pans stopped rattling.

"I said, who's over there?"

Still there was no reply.

"I've got two barrels of a shotgun pointed across the camp. Identify yourself or you'll get both barrels."

"Cookie! Wait! It's me—Felix. I'm just digging for a little sugar for my coffee."

"Get away from that wagon or I'll bust open your worthless skull. There ain't no old boy on this green earth that's digging in my wagon. You got that?"

"Relax, you cranky old man, I—"

Brannon heard a thud and a yelp.

"Hey . . . you almost hit me with that knife!"

"A mistake I won't make again!"

"I have half a mind to lead you down right now."

"I doubt if you even have half a mind," the cook spat out. "Get on out of here!"

Brannon heard the man stomp across off to the east. He waited.

Suddenly, a lantern lit at the far side of the chuck wagon. Brannon rolled back into the shadows. The bearded face of an older man appeared in the reflected light as he shuffled toward the wagon.

They must be born that way. All chuck wagon cooks look exactly the same!

After a quick inspection of his cupboards, the cook walked to the front of the wagon, opened the canvas flap, and pulled out another lantern. He filled the second lantern with kerosene and then stuck the jug back into the wagon. He turned the one lantern off, and Brannon could hear him make his way back across the campsite.

The front door's open and kerosene's inside. Couldn't ask for anything better than that!

Brannon now worked quickly in the dark. He pulled out the two sticks of dynamite. Then, lying on his back, he took his knife and poked a deep hole in the end of the dynamite. Cutting the fuse to about a foot and a half in length, he gingerly crimped the blasting cap to the fuse by biting it with his teeth. Finally he shoved the cap and fuse into the hole in the dynamite and gently tamped it in place.

With both sticks prepared, he slowly inched his way closer to the front of the wagon. At about ten feet, he sat up, stuck his gun back into his belt, and practiced the throw towards the wagon. He was tempted to light the dynamite and get the action started.

I am not a violent man. I will not start this fight.

Brannon waited for what seemed like an hour. Then, suddenly, torches flared up completely surrounding the ranch house.

There must be twenty torches!

Instantly, he sat up and lit both sticks of dynamite. He heard the reports of gunfire echoing up from the ranch. When the fuses started to glow and sparkle, he tossed both sticks into the front of the wagon, turned, and dove for the weeds. With his face close to the dirt, he crawled back towards the piñons.

The explosions rocked the ground and banged hard against Brannon's eardrums. He whipped around to see a double burst of flames, and then supplies flew through the air in every direction. Bits and pieces of burning material littered the whole camp, dispatching little scraps of flame and debris. What was left of the wagon, mainly the utensil box, wheels, and water barrels, now caught fire and crackled in the mountain breeze.

As he heard men rushing toward the burning wagon, he redoubled his efforts to reach the graves. Out of breath, his raw hand bleeding, his ducking worn clear through at the right knee, he finally reached the two piñons.

He collapsed against the base of a tree as he heard the shouts of men around the chuck wagon, but the sight that captured his attention was ten-foot flames leaping from the top of his house.

I've got to get those women out of there and back to Prescott!

The Collectors near the campsite were busy fighting their own fire and occasionally taking shots at the shadows. Staying wide of the main route back to the house and keeping low in the weeds, Brannon crawled on his hands and knees back to the ranch. He could hear shouts and see men running back up the hill towards camp. In the confusion some of the Collectors shot at each other.

Again and again Brannon tumbled in the rocks and grass and rolled through the dirt. His right foot was completely numb and wouldn't support any weight at all. He wrapped his bandanna around the palm of his bleeding hand and scurried the best he could down the hill.

Lord, don't let those ladies get hurt! It's my fault. Don't let them pay . . . I couldn't live with that!

Halfway down the hill he rolled over in the grass and lay on his back, puffing. The gunfire continued in the Collectors' camp, but he could no longer hear any from the ranch headquarters. He thought he could see people on the roof of the house, and the flames seemed to be dying back a little.

By the time he reached the barn, he could see no flames at all, but a thick cloud of smoke filled the yard. He yanked up the loose board and scooted into the barn.

"Harvey? Gonzales?" he called.

There was no reply.

Grabbing his hat and the crutch, Brannon hopped, stumbled, and staggered towards the house.

"Stuart?" Miss Cancino called from the porch.

"Yeah . . . where's everyone?"

Earl Howland stepped out into the yard. "Around back."

"How in the world did you get that fire out?"

"The soldiers formed a bucket brigade. Fortunately your diversion worked, and half of them tossed down their torches and ran back up to camp."

"We kept them from coming into the yard, so they could only get close back there," Julie added.

"Anyone get hurt?"

"Fletcher's up on the roof somewhere."

"Earl, post Harvey and Gonzales back at the outbuildings in case they get mad and rush back down here. Miss Cancino, are you safe on the porch?"

"Safe? No one's safe being within ten miles of you, Stuart Brannon. But I'll be all right."

Brannon could hear shouts in the back of the house. He pushed his way through the smoky living room and into the back bedrooms. A lantern cast a dreamy look about the place as shadowy bodies coughed their way through the rooms.

"Brannon," Sergeant Cloverdale shouted, "that was quite an explosion."

"Stuart, Edwin's trapped on the roof!" Harriet yelled.

"Is he shot?"

"I don't think so."

"Burnt?"

"No . . . just stuck! He fell through. He crawled up there with a wet quilt to fight the flames, and the roof collapsed under him. His feet are dangling down in the bedroom."

Several soldiers milled around the outside of the house, trying to decide how to rescue the Englishman.

"Edwin? Can you hear me?"

"Brannon? I say—I'd prefer not to stay in this position all night."

"The rest of the roof collapsed, and there doesn't seem to be a way to get over to you," Brannon shouted.

"Well, my word, think of something!"

"Are you straddling any timbers?"

"No, I'm just holding on with my arms."

"Listen, when I tug on your foot, you hold your hands straight above your head."

Brannon went into the bedroom. Burnt timbers and shingles littered a wet bed. Fletcher's feet swung about a foot above Brannon's outstretched arms.

Brannon began to cough.

"Nelson, you and Mrs. Barton open all the windows in the house. Sergeant, bring a couple other men and come in here."

The soldiers crowded into the little back bedroom.

"Hoist me up there." He pointed to Fletcher's legs.

They grabbed Brannon and lifted him straight up until he could lock his arms around Fletcher's feet.

"Now drop me!" he shouted.

They did.

The weight of Brannon on his legs unwedged Fletcher, and the two men crashed onto the soaking wet bed, which promptly collapsed. They rolled to the floor.

Brannon lay staring upward, completely exhausted.

"Drag us out of here, Sergeant!" he shouted.

Within moments, all of them except for a guard or two were on the front porch.

Propped up on the bench beside Miss Cancino, Brannon sucked up the fresh air and coughed his lungs clear.

"Earl, at the first hint of dawn, I want you to hitch up those two carriages. Folks, this is the end of the line. I am grateful for your support, but sitting up there on that hillside tonight, watching the roof blaze up, I realized that I would rather die than have to bury another woman in those piñons.

"Sergeant, the first thing in the morning, I want you and your men to escort these folks out of the valley. Earl, I'll pay you a month's wages, but you should ride with the soldiers. I think you can make it, too. Edwin, this is a good time for you to take another jaunt to San Francisco."

"I say, Brannon—"

"Look, I don't want to be dramatic or sound like Martin Luther, but everyone comes to a place in their life when they say, 'This is it . . . here I stand. God help me.' Well, this ranch is my place. I lost everything I ever valued right in this house. When I die, I'm going to die right here. But I'm not going to put you through another battle. You have already suffered more than enough."

"Are you through with your speech, Mr. Brannon?" Earl Howland asked.

"I'm through."

"Well, I ain't leavin'," Howland reported. "You promised me twenty cows and a bull. I aim to make a ranch out of that, and I'll build myself a house and a barn, and then if I can get the nerve, I'm going ask Miss Julie to marry me. And you and all your fancy talkin' aren't going to cheat me out of that."

"Earl, the odds aren't very good that I can deliver on that promise."

"I'll take my chance."

"I'm not leaving either," Miss Cancino added.

"Look," Brannon huffed, "I didn't ask you if you wanted to leave. I will not put ladies in danger again!"

"Oh, save it, Brannon," she retorted. "You try to throw me out of this ranch and I'll shoot you in the other foot. If you get too dramatic, I'll get out the violins and remind you how it is that my legs are paralyzed! I want to stay. A girl who can't walk across the room isn't going to get many better offers than I just had."

"This doesn't make sense," Brannon protested. "You have to get out of here!"

"Stuart," Harriet began, "I think you really should allow—"

"Miss Reed, don't you begin on me. I have no intention of allowing—"

"Mr. Brannon," she shouted, "in the past few days I have been shot at, roped, dragged through the dirt, nearly burnt alive, soaked to the bone in water. I do not have with me one, not one, stitch of clothing that could be worn at any civilized function. I do not know what the future holds—whether I will be slaughtered by savage Indians, shot by marauders, burned alive in a barn, or die as an elderly tottering rancher's widow. But I am not going to go back and sit on the front porch of a Victorian home and crochet doilies! Is that understood?"

"This is insane . . . it's not your battle," he pleaded at Barton.

"Gwen and I are not exactly the heroic type that you stir up in others."

"I stir up?"

"But there is something heroic going on here. We came out to this country to contribute something that would help to settle this land. We wanted to be an active part in helping Arizona achieve statehood. We wanted to give our efforts to something that would make a difference. Well, a country ruled by armed bands of men will never be a settled land. We'd like to make our stand right here. It's not for you . . . it's for the whole Territory, for the next generation."

"It has a tinge of the historic, Mr. Brannon," Gwendolyn added. "I don't mean to sound theatric, but we want to see what happens here."

In desperation, Brannon glanced at Gonzales and Harvey. "Men, you get to—"

"Mr. Brannon," Harvey said with a heavy Texas drawl, "my granddaddy rode with old Sam Houston at San Jacinto. He always said it changed his life something permanent. Well, this isn't east Texas, and you're not Mr. Houston, but it just might be as close as I get. Someday I want to look back and say, 'I fought alongside Stuart Brannon at Sunrise Creek.'"

"I'm with Harvey," Gonzales added. "If I ride out now, I'll

spend the rest of my life wondering what would have happened if I'd stayed."

"Listen . . . I'm not making myself clear . . . Edwin, explain—"

"Just face it, man. You can't chase them off. You can't chase any of us off. Everyone here has his own motive for sticking it out. We aren't doing it just for you. We're doing it for ourselves. You, of all people, Stuart, know that life is seldom rational!"

"Look, they'll come back and next time they'll—"

"I say, we really must put Brannon to bed. He's mumbling on and on in incoherent phrases."

"Sergeant . . . ?" Brannon appealed.

"We must stay until my messenger comes back from Prescott with orders. It's strictly a military decision. Of course, several of the men figure that if they stick it out, they might warrant a mention in the next dime novel."

"They what?" Brannon shouted.

"Relax." Cloverdale broke into a grin. "If your goal in life was to die a lonely martyr, you're out of luck. It looks like we're all staying."

Within the hour they resumed their positions, with Brannon on the front porch sitting next to Cancino and Reed.

"You ladies should go inside. Try to get some sleep," Brannon insisted.

"Our room is full of smoke, the roof caved in, and the bed is broken and soaked with water," Harriet reminded him. "We'll just sit out here if you don't mind." She stepped into the house and re-emerged with a quilt which she tucked around Miss Cancino and herself.

After several moments of silence, Miss Reed spoke up. "Stuart . . . is this a battle between good and evil?"

"You mean—in a spiritual sense?"

"Yes."

"I wish I knew. There's nothing evil about a valid land grant. But something is wrong with private armies that use threats and coercion to extort money."

"Well, I would like to think that we've made a stand for good."

"It's not always easy to discern, is it? Jedel and his type are simple to categorize, but when I'm honest, well . . . I wonder if I would ever let this place go, even if God Almighty told me to directly. Being on the side of 'good,' fighting so-called 'evil' has probably disguised a lot of selfish intentions."

"God will assist us if we're right," she offered.

"And forgive us, I hope, if we're wrong," Brannon added.

"He is generous to forgive."

"Miss Harriet, it is that one attribute of the Lord that gives me constant hope. It's what keeps me plugging away during the day and allows me to rest at night."

"Stuart! Wake up! Look up there! Isn't that a wagon on the road?"

Brannon jumped up from the chair. This time, instead of collapsing on his injured foot, he was able to stagger across the porch to the rail.

Daylight had just broken in the east. Brannon rubbed his eyes and stared into the distance.

"It's a wagon . . . some kind of wagon."

Fletcher hiked across the yard from the bunkhouse. "What do you make of it?"

"Let's go check with Cloverdale. He's got the spyglass."

By resting his right hand on Fletcher's shoulder, Brannon managed to hobble to the soldiers' quarters. Within moments, Cloverdale was out of his tent and scoping the new arrival.

"It's those two men who left last week with Jedel . . . Oh, no!" he groaned.

"What is it?" Brannon quizzed.

"A cannon."

"A cannon? You mean a—"

"I mean a cannon. They can sit up there and lob shells into any of these buildings!"

"But people don't own cannons, do they?"

"They do now."

"Maybe they're just trying to scare us," Fletcher offered.

"Well, it's working!" Brannon rubbed the stubble of his three-day beard.

"This has gone far enough," Cloverdale huffed. "We'll have to confiscate that weapon."

"Do you have the manpower?" Fletcher questioned.

"That remains to be seen. Until I develop a plan, I want to station men throughout the ranch yard. I want my men in every location and highly visible. Any shot fired will be have to aimed straight at the U. S. Army."

After breakfast, Brannon, Fletcher, and Cloverdale sat on the front porch to finalize plans.

"There's no easy way to do it," Brannon repeated. "If they want to shoot it out, lots of men are going to die."

"If they fire on government troops, they're finished in Arizona. It would defeat their purpose," Cloverdale offered.

"No," Brannon cautioned, "it would defeat Burlingame's purpose. Some of these men care little for land grants that will belong to someone else. They just want to win the battle today."

"We'll find out which soon enough." Cloverdale paced with his hands clutched behind his back. "There's no reason to hesitate any longer. We'll—"

"Sergeant!"

One of the soldiers sprinted to the ranch house. "Sergeant, troops are coming!"

Cloverdale trotted out to the middle of the yard.

"Up the trail to the north . . . look!" He shoved the spyglass towards the sergeant.

"It's Captain Wells!"

"I say," Fletcher mumbled, "that is rather good timing!"

"Like an answer to prayer," Brannon added.

ELEVEN

Everyone except Julie Cancino stood in front of the half-burnt ranch house as Captain Wells led fifty-six men into the yard.

"I knew it would work out. I just knew it!" Cancino bubbled.

"Like the ending of a good novel," Reed admitted. "Just when all is lost—the heroes arrive to save the day."

"Gives you a little hope for this land, doesn't it?" Nelson Barton sighed.

"What do you think, Stuart?" Fletcher put in.

"I don't think anybody sent troops to save this ranch," he muttered.

"That would be highly doubtful," Cloverdale agreed. He stepped out to meet the captain.

After a long discussion, Wells dismounted, but kept the rest of his troops horseback. They walked over to Brannon.

"Mr. Brannon," the sergeant announced, "this is Captain Wells . . . and we need to talk privately on this situation."

Brannon nodded toward the corrals.

"Sorry for being so slow, Captain. I took a shot in my foot. This has been the first day I've been able to stick it in a boot."

"Mr. Brannon, I'll be very blunt. I understand the urgency of your situation. But I have been ordered to withdraw Sergeant Cloverdale and the troops. We have been assigned to pursue the Apaches over the mountains and back to the reservation."

"Captain, we've got women here!"

"Brannon, the sergeant has informed me of the arrival of artillery, and I am quite aware of the context of all of this. Most everyone in the Territory is. But my orders have come from the War Department. When we all signed on, we agreed to follow orders."

"What do you mean, 'everyone in the Territory'?" Brannon quizzed.

"You have seen the newspapers, haven't you?"

"I haven't seen a paper in a month."

Captain Wells turned and shouted to the troops, "Lieutenant, bring me my saddlebags!"

While they waited, Brannon renewed the conversation. "If you have to leave, you must escort the ladies out of here."

"I can't even do that," the captain informed him. "We're headed right up Sunrise Creek, and I have specific instructions not to pursue any action that might be construed as taking sides in the Yavapai County War."

"The what?"

"They're calling it the Yavapai County War."

"Who's calling it that?" Brannon bellowed.

"The newspapers." Taking the saddlebags from the lieutenant, he pulled out several clippings. Here's one from the *Florence Enterprise* and another from the *Prescott Miner*. I understand they've sent the story to San Francisco, New York, Chicago, and Washington, DC."

"Tom Weedin in Florence?"

"Yes, he wrote the initial story based on information from Judge and Mrs. Quilici. He paints quite a picture of your heroic struggle against the Collectors. Here. Look at this."

Brannon read aloud:

"Veteran Indian fighter and lawman, Stuart Brannon, is in the battle of his life as he stands off Casa Verde Land Development Corporation's army of so-called 'Collectors.' Trapped on his Triple B Ranch near the mouth of Sunrise Creek, Brannon and several other prominent Arizona citi-

zens are holding off the hired guns that support Burlingame's
claim to the spurious DePalma-Revera grant . . ."

"And here's one from the *Miner*." The captain handed him
another clipping.
"Yavapai County War?"

"Stuart Brannon, A. T. pioneer cattleman, has drawn the line
against the Collectors, refusing to succumb to their extortion
. . . undoubtedly the action along little Sunrise Creek will be
heard all the way to the hallowed halls of Congress. Perhaps,
at last, they will move to settle these land grant matters."

Brannon just stared at the papers.
The captain gestured. "Mr. Brannon, you are free to keep those
if you'd like. It seems your friends, Judge and Mrs. Quilici, are
determined to force the Surveyor-General to come up and investigate this situation. The notoriety certainly is gaining you support
in the Territory. However, Mr. Burlingame has friends in
Washington . . . and I presume they're responsible for my orders.
I assure you I have no other choice."

Sergeant Cloverdale stepped closer to Brannon. "Stuart, I flat
told the captain that I didn't think my men would want to abandon their position, but I was informed that if we didn't follow
orders, we would be locked in irons and hauled back to the barracks for court-martial."

"Sergeant, I completely understand your predicament. Go
ahead and strike camp. I'll tell the others. Captain Wells, I wish
you well in your pursuit of the Apaches. On some other day, I
would volunteer to lead you through the mountains."
"Good day, Mr. Brannon, and good luck."
It will take considerably more than luck.
Brannon hobbled back to the house and the waiting crowd.
"I say," Fletcher called, "where are the soldiers going?"
"To help Cloverdale strike camp," Brannon called.
"Good heavens, are they leaving?"
"Yep."

"Are you serious?" Mr. Barton roared.

Gripping the newspaper clippings in one hand, he motioned for them to pull in closer. For the next ten minutes he tried tô explain.

Harriet Reed broke the depressing silence, "Well, we were right about the significance of this event."

"Shall we pack up and ride out of here now?" Fletcher asked.

"It's too late for that," Miss Cancino replied.

Brannon said softly, "I want them to fire the cannon."

"You what?" Reed exclaimed.

"I want the records to show that it took a small army and an artillery piece to drive Stuart Brannon from his land."

"And how do we stay alive in the process?" Fletcher pressed.

"That's what we'll have to determine. They won't use it with the army in view, so we have a little time."

In less than an hour, Cloverdale and men had packed camp and joined the captain and his troops. The sergeant rode by Brannon and the others.

"I have seriously considered the cost of being court-martialed, but I must confess I am afraid to face that fate. Besides, locked in irons, I would be of no help to you. Mr. Brannon, I believe you might need this more than I."

He handed Brannon his spyglass.

"Sergeant, thanks for the loan. I will return it to you the next time I'm up in Prescott."

Sergeant Cloverdale gaped for a moment.

"I will look forward to that meeting," he concluded.

They all watched in silence as the long column of troops left the yard and began the climb up the valley floor alongside Sunrise Creek.

"Kind of like clutching the rail of a sinking ship and watching your only lifeboat go down," Fletcher murmured.

"How long do you suppose until they fire that weapon?" Barton pondered.

"Several hours, I reckon," Brannon offered. "Look, I want us to abandon the bunk and the barn. The house has thick adobe walls and a fairly good root cellar. We'll use it for protection."

"I'm not leaving the front porch," Julie Cancino insisted. "I want those fifty men to know that they're shooting those cannon balls right at a crippled woman."

"I'm staying with Miss Julie," Howland added.

Harriet Reed slapped her hands to her hips. "We're all in this together. So let's just sit out here and give them a target."

"I've got a feeling," Brannon continued, "that we won't be the first target. They'll aim for the bunkhouse, hoping we'll flee once we see the damage they can do."

Gwen Barton inquired, "Then we'll be safe if we stay by the house?"

"If they know how to use that thing. If they don't, who knows where a shell might land," Brannon cautioned.

The sky was clear, and a light breeze from the northwest blew most of the morning. They stacked cordwood about four feet tall in front of the porch, opened the root cellar for possible use under attack, and distributed their weapons around the perimeter of their defenses. Even though the hours were spent in preparation for battle, Brannon noticed a light, almost reckless attitude in everyone.

It was Fletcher who commented on the situation. "Really, Brannon, it's almost like a game. The women giggle; the men (who have probably never dodged a bullet in their lives) joke about bravery. Harriet's recording everything for a book; Howland is making plans as to where his ranch should be. Julie's begging us to hold her up so she can practice walking. Don't they realize that in a matter of hours we could all be dead?"

"They know that, Edwin . . . they're just scared. So you cover it up with levity. It's better than tears and sorrow."

"Do you ever seriously think about death, Brannon?"

"My own?"

"Yes."

"I use to . . . but I guess I don't anymore."

"Why not?"

"Well, there's two reasons to be afraid of dying. You can be afraid because you don't know what happens after death. But the way I got it figured, the crucifixion and the empty tomb solved that dilemma—if we'd only trust in it."

"You said there were two problems."

"Well, some people are afraid of death because of what they have to give up here on earth. They can't bear to think about being separated from loved ones and of all the experiences they'll miss. I guess, for me, death would be a reunion, not a separation."

"Lisa and the baby?"

"Yep."

"It never heals, does it?"

"Nope."

The June sun was halfway down the western sky when Howland hollered from the barn loft, "Mr. Brannon! They're loadin' up that cannon!"

"Is it pointed this way?"

"Yeah."

"Bring that spyglass and come on down out of there!"

"Where do you want us to be?" Reed called.

"In Prescott."

"Stuart!"

"Look, any of you who want can file into that root cellar."

"It won't matter all that much." Nelson Barton shrugged. "We might as well watch from the porch together."

"Well, Stuart," Harriet said with a sigh, "you certainly know how to entertain guests!"

Brannon put his right hand on Howland's shoulder. "Earl, keep a scope on that cannon. I want to know if they immediately load up another round, or start charging down the hill, or whatever."

"Yes, sir. It looks like Jedel with the torch. Hang on, folks, here it comes . . . somethin's wrong!"

Just as Howland shouted, Brannon heard a tremendous explosion. He and the others ducked down behind the stacks of firewood.

"Where is it?" Reed called.

"Is it still coming in?"

"What happened?"

"Over there . . . look!" Someone pointed to the other side of Sunrise Creek.

"They hit a cottonwood tree!"

"On the other side of the creek?"

"That's over a half-mile away!"

"Look at this! Mr. Brannon, look at this!" Howland thrust the spyglass into his hands.

"It busted up! Looks like the cannon lost a wheel and broke loose from the mounts!"

Suddenly a sense of immediate relief swept across their faces. They hollered and hugged.

"The Lord did it! He broke their cannon," Harriet proclaimed.

It was Brannon who quieted them down.

"Folks . . . even without that cannon, it's the same men who burnt down half the ranch last night. And now we don't have the soldiers. We survived this round, but, to quote the papers, the war isn't over. We'd better get ready for the next round."

"Are you going to crawl back up there tonight?"

"Nope, Earl, it would be too dangerous now. But we might use some half sticks of that dynamite to drive them back up the hill."

"How'll we know when they're comin' down?"

"A trip wire will sound the alarm."

"What alarm?"

"Caterwauling when they stumble into that fancy new wire you brought me."

"We going to put up a fence?"

"Nope, just a small barrier."

"What good would that do? They can go right over it."

"If they knew it was there."

"What are we going to do, put it up after dark?"

"Yep."

It was Fletcher who now held the spyglass. "Looks like they might be trying to repair the cannon."

"They're going to fire that thing again?" Harriet asked.

"Probably not before tomorrow," Brannon suggested. "Let today's trouble be sufficient for today. Right now, you ladies have got to do something about those dresses. You look frightful."

"Well, I'm glad you noticed," Reed said with a shrug, "but now's hardly the time to . . . "

Brannon jammed his sleeves above his elbows and pointed at Reed. "That's where you're wrong! I think we should all dress up with our finest. Tonight we have a banquet."

"Are you serious?"

"Serious? No, it's frivolous. That's why we need to do it!" Brannon asserted. "Mrs. Barton, could you be in charge of meal preparation?"

"Why . . . yes, Mr. Brannon. The kitchen is still in working condition. But, really . . . I don't—"

"And nothing's wrong with the dining room," Brannon added. "After all, we have a lot to celebrate."

"Oh?" Harriet Reed raised an eyebrow.

"We're all alive and . . ."

"And what?" Cancino asked.

"And if Howland gets off his duff, he and Julie will have something to announce to us."

"Stuart!" Harriet cautioned.

"Do you understand, Earl?" Brannon pressed.

"Yes, sir, I do. And I aim to take care of that this afternoon."

"Well, that still doesn't solve the problem of our—what was the word? Frightful appearance?"

"Miss Reed, you and the ladies go search through that cedar chest in the corner of the living room. Should be a dress or two there, and I've got a feeling they're going fit you just fine."

"Are they Lisa's?"

"Yep."

"We couldn't—"

"Harriet, by morning everything in this house could be burnt to the ground. It would be a tragedy to never see those dresses on pretty ladies again. I would appreciate it if you would give them a try."

"Very well, we'll look into them. But we expect you men to do the same! And," she continued, "you better pull what you need out of the house because until supper this is off limits to men."

Brannon left Howland on the porch with Miss Cancino and the

spyglass, with instructions to shout a warning if the Collectors began to move down the mountain toward the ranch buildings. Then he and the other men surveyed the grounds and planned their defenses for the night.

"Really, Brannon, why this charade?" Fletcher queried.

"Diversion."

"Us or them?"

"Both. Maybe we can get our minds off this constant anticipation—and maybe convince the Collectors that we have let down our guard."

"Which we won't?"

"Precisely. We've got to stop them before they burn any buildings, because I don't think we've got the manpower to put out another fire."

"How about the wire?" Nelson Barton questioned.

"Edwin and I will string it right after dark."

"We will?"

"Sure, it's part of the plan."

"What plan?"

"I'll let you know, Edwin . . . as soon as I have one!"

By the late afternoon, the men had done their best to scrub and shave, and all but Brannon were wearing coats and ties. He had given his only dress coat and tie to Earl Howland.

"Mr. Brannon, I don't know why I should wear this and you don't have to."

"Did you ask her?"

"Yes, sir, I did."

"And what did she say?"

"She said yes!"

"So when's the big day?"

"After we drive those cows up from Mexico and I build her a house. I figure it will be next spring. Is that all right with you, Mr. Brannon?"

"Earl, this has absolutely nothing to do with me. But it sounds fine."

Supper was finally ready. Gwendolyn Barton appeared at the door and invited the men inside. Gonzales and Harvey volunteered to take turns out on the porch scoping the Collectors in case of a raid.

"You look very nice in that dress, Mrs. Barton," Brannon remarked.

"Thank you, Stuart. Your Lisa certainly had some lovely things."

"They always said she had good taste in everything but husbands," he laughed. "And, Miss Julie, is it symbolic that you chose the white dress?"

"Harriet picked it out for me. This material is so smooth it makes me feel really special."

"You look stunning," Fletcher declared.

"She looks good all the time," Howland added.

Brannon turned to see Harriet Reed stroll into the dining room. *I knew she would wear the rose dress . . . it was bound to happen.* Memories flooded through his mind, and he had a strong urge to hold Miss Reed in his arms.

"Well," she said, "is this dress less frightful?"

"Miss Reed, it's ravishing!" Fletcher called out.

"Stuart . . . are you all right?" she pressed.

"Harriet, you remind me of someone . . . and I really appreciate the memories!"

"That's it? My word, Brannon, that's not much of a compliment," Fletcher complained.

"No, Mr. Fletcher," Reed protested, "it is the ultimate of compliments from Stuart. And I am flattered that he would offer it to me."

Except for the occasional report from the scout on the front porch, the party was lighthearted and the time flew by quickly. The laughter, Brannon knew, was shallow—but needed.

You make a lot of plans for the future when you aren't sure if you'll make it through the night. No idea is too wild, no scheme too irrational, no dream too absurd.

One by one he surveyed the guests in his house.

Lord, this is what was missing after Lisa died. People . . . laugh-

ter . . . excitement . . . that's what I want this place to be. T[...]st enjoyable stop between Prescott and Tucson. I don't k[...] to do that on my own, Lord. Lisa could do it. Wouldn't [...] e with a group like this? . . . wouldn't she have shined?

As the sun began to set, Brannon signaled for their attention.

"I don't want to spoil our party, but it's about time to go to work. Here's what we do. As soon as it's dark, Edwin and I will crawl—"

"I say . . . crawl?"

"You can change clothes, of course. Then we'll station ourselves out there with the dynamite. Since we've used it in the mine, we'll take that detail."

"What do you want us to do?" Earl asked.

"I want you to keep laughing, singing, dancing. Make them think that we're totally unconcerned with their activity."

Brannon pulled his black hat off a peg in the wall and shoved it down on Howland's head.

"Earl, you stay by the window. In the shadows you'll look like old man Brannon himself."

"So they can shoot at him?" Cancino challenged.

"I don't think so. They must still have orders not to ride in with guns blazing. But if they think I'm in here, they won't expect me out there. We only need to fool them for a while."

"So we just live it up inside?"

"Right. At the first blast from a gun or dynamite, shut off the lanterns and take your positions."

"What if they don't come down tonight?"

"Then it'll be a long party. I just don't think this will be the worst night. By tomorrow they'll either straighten out the aim on the cannon or they'll roar down that mountain."

"But . . . if things turn out badly, well, as Edwin knows, I've spent most of the past two years fighting other people's battles. And now . . . it feels good to fight one of my own. But I couldn't have done it without you."

"Stuart, go stretch your wire before we change our minds," Reed needled.

Working on their hands and knees, Brannon and Fletcher cordoned off the yard with a strand of barbed wire stretched about a foot above the ground. Back in the barn, they each set six half sticks of dynamite and stuffed them in their pockets.

"Well, Edwin, do you ever think of just riding out of here, catching a schooner around the Horn, and going home?"

"Stuart, life with you has spoiled me for anything else. I sat at a formal dinner in San Francisco last week. For two hours the ambassador from Russia tried to explain why the $7,200,000 paid for Alaska was far too cheap a price, and I realized that all I could think about was riding down into Mexico and buying a thousand head of cattle. This land makes you think, feel, reason, and act quickly. Anything else is just coasting."

"Well, Lord Fletcher, let's go to work."

"Quite right."

"Edwin, you stay at the corner of the barn. If you hear them on the north or east, go to it. Just don't throw them too close to the house."

"You know, Brannon, they are going to come in from the south . . . or maybe the west."

"Yeah . . . I know. That's why I'm down there. Here, have a cigar."

"A cigar? Where did you get these?"

"From Barton."

"I don't smoke. Brannon, you don't smoke!"

"For the fuses. Lay it on the ground, and it's hardly visible. A match flares up too much."

For an hour Brannon sat with his back to a cottonwood tree in the front yard, waiting to hear sounds of intruders.

If they find the wire and go over it, they'll be on top of us before we can act. Lord, help us!

Suddenly, Brannon sensed movement on the hill.

He couldn't see anything.

He couldn't hear anything.

But he knew they were moving.

He glanced down and relit the cigar. Then he laid all six half sticks of dynamite out in a row beside him. Holding one in his right hand only a few inches above the glowing cigar, he waited . . . and waited . . . and waited.

Then it came.

Straight from the south.

A scream.

A shout.

A curse.

And shots fired wildly.

He lit the dynamite and tossed it with all his might.

The explosion lit up terrified and confused faces. He threw another to the same place, then lit another, and tossed it to the west.

Blasts rang out from the north as Fletcher contributed to the mayhem. Brannon tossed two more. He could see men scrambling back up the hill. Pulling himself to his feet, he staggered toward the fleeing men, lit another stick, and heaved it far into the dark night.

Suddenly, he saw a glowing object fly in his direction.

They had thrown it back!

He dove for the cottonwood and rolled behind it, hands clamped over his ears. But the explosion was not as close as he had feared. In fact, in the confusion the fleeing Collector had completely missed his target. The dynamite fell just under the front steps of the bunkhouse.

The explosion sent splinters clear across the yard. The front door of the bunkhouse blazed. He wanted to run put the fire out, but realized if any men were still close, his silhouette against the flames would make an easy target. Several gunshots were fired randomly at the house, and then the shouts and cursing ceased.

"I say, Brannon?"

"Edwin? Over here!"

"My word, aren't we going to try to save that building?"

"Nope. It's too dangerous. Let it burn."

"Did they sneak up and torch it?"

"Nope."

"What happened?"

"Dynamite. They threw a stick back!"

"Good heavens, we were fortunate they only hit the bunkhouse."

"That's what I was thinking."

"Will they return?"

"I don't think so. But pass the word to keep the posts all night long."

Right before dawn, Fletcher and Brannon and Howland crawled out and took down the barbed wire. They dragged it back into the barn and then joined the others on the porch. The ladies still wore their party dresses.

"It's a beautiful morning, Mr. Brannon," Julie greeted him.

"Yes, it is. Every morning you're alive is beautiful, isn't it?"

Harriet Reed walked up to Brannon and slipped her arm in his. "You know, I believe I have enough material for a whole series of books. But I'm going to have to call it fiction."

Brannon liked the feel of her arm in his and the rustle of the rose dress next to him. "Why's that?" he asked.

"Because no one would believe that it's true. Come on. Gwen's fixing breakfast."

"Mr. Brannon!" Earl Howland yelled. "You better take a look at this. Some guy just pulled up to the top of the rim in a buckboard and—and . . ." His voice trailed off.

"And what?"

"I think they fixed the cannon!"

"Get behind those barriers!" Brannon shouted commands. "If they hit the house, they'll charge down immediately afterward. Go for Jedel. The others are just hired hands!"

A distant puff of smoke, then an ear-banging report, followed by an explosion behind the house.

"They missed! They overshot!" Cancino hollered.

"Earl, run around and see what kind of damage was done!" Brannon called.

Fletcher manned the spyglass. "They're loading again . . . no . . . no, something's wrong . . . they can't get it loaded."

"It's too hot. They used too much powder. They'll have to let it cool off."

Howland sprinted back. "Mr. Brannon! They hit the privy!"

"The privy? The old one or the new one?"

"The new one. It's nothing but a pile of splinters!"

"Fortunately, they don't seem to know how to aim that thing," Nelson Barton interjected.

"I don't know." Brannon shrugged. "Maybe that was their target. It could add a certain urgency to settle this matter."

"There's more of them, Stuart!" Fletcher called out from behind the spyglass.

"More Collectors?"

"No, more wagons up on the rim. My word, it looks like women, children, men—whole families!"

TWELVE

Families?" Brannon took the spyglass.

"Look up at the north road. I think someone's up there too!" Reed called out.

Brannon switched his scope to the other side of the valley.

"I see them! Several riders, a freight wagon, a carriage—there's a stagecoach! How in the world did they get a stage up that goat path? And there's a tent. They must have come in last night."

"What are they doing here?" Fletcher inquired.

"Maybe they're bringing supplies to the Collectors," Cancino suggested.

Brannon handed the spyglass back to Howland and turned to the others.

"I don't know what's going on. There are some women and children on that south rim. Maybe . . . maybe Casa Verde is bringing in squatters to show a land feud rather than a battle of hired guns. It's crazy. At this rate the Triple B will be the third largest town in the Territory by nightfall."

Suddenly Howland shouted, "This is it! I think they're coming down."

"The wagons?"

"No, the Collectors. They're all tossing on saddles."

Brannon rubbed his grimy forehead and pushed back his hat. "Well, let's get ready for them. Get to your positions, check your ammunition, load your guns to the maximum. Ladies, you'll need to—"

"Mr. Brannon, do you have any clothesline rope?" Reed asked.

"Have any what?"

"Clothesline rope. I want to wash out a few things and hang them up in the yard," she replied.

"Is this a joke?"

"Stuart, as you all know, I am next to useless at shooting anything except a horse. So I believe I can serve us best by standing unarmed in the middle of the yard, doing my laundry."

"Brannon," Fletcher blurted, "remember Janie Mulroney? Perhaps Miss Reed has also broken down under the pressure."

"No! You're right, Harriet! Can't you see, Edwin?"

"I say—another diversion?"

"No, no! We're surrounded by witnesses! How can they shoot at unarmed women doing their chores? If we look like a fort, if we fire at them, they'll claim to have an excuse for attacking. This is an ordinary working ranch, and that's what we'll be."

"An ordinary ranch with half the house burnt down, the bunkhouse in ashes, and a privy blown to shreds," Fletcher added.

"Look," Brannon shouted, "carry your weapon out of sight, but go about your business. Hurry, ladies, bring out your wash. Nelson, string a line across the front yard. Gonzales and Harvey, start cleaning up around the bunkhouse."

"What do you want me to do?" Howland asked.

"Pull a couple horses out of the corral and begin to groom them. Take your time. Act like nothing is going on."

"I'll heat up the forge and pound out some horseshoes in front of the barn."

"And me?" Fletcher asked.

"Eh . . . well, you sit out there in the middle of the yard with Julie and read."

"Read? My word, Brannon, you don't expect us to—"

Miss Cancino called out, "Read to all of us!"

"Oh, all right, but it does seem terribly loose," Fletcher protested.

Within minutes the whole crew was in place, each one visible to the people on the north and south rim as well as to the Collectors.

"Here they come," Julie Cancino shouted. "Read, Mr. Fletcher! Read!"

"Fate had brought Odysseus to the Kingdom of the Phaeacians. On the island where he had set foot stood their city with the palace of King Alcinous, father of young Nausicaa. She was in the full bloom of youth, slender and lithe like a reed and very beautiful . . ."

"I say, this is rather—"

"Read it, Fletcher!" Brannon shouted.

"They stopped, Mr. Brannon!" Howland called out. "They stopped about halfway down the slope. The wagons are rolling! Those folks from up top are coming down too!"

"So are the ones on the north rim," Harriet called out. "Everyone's coming down here!"

"What do we do now, Brannon?" Fletcher asked.

Lord, this is . . . eh, this is . . . Are they coming just to watch us get shot? Lord, I'm not a violent man, but I'm getting to be an angry one. Whatever happened to my peaceful little ranch?

The Collectors waited for the wagons to pass and then fell in line behind them. Brannon had a strong desire to grab up his Winchester and meet the first wagon with rifle in hand. But instead he dropped an extra Colt into his coat pocket and walked across the yard, waiting for the string of wagons.

It took a long while for everyone to reach the ranch house, and even as they circled the outside of the place, Brannon noticed other rigs rolling down the mountains from the north and the south.

"Hello, Mr. Brannon!" one wagon driver shouted.

He turned but didn't recognize the man.

Julie waved at a wagon. "There's some of the girls from the Lucky Dollar!"

The first man to actually enter the yard parked his wagon beyond the burnt-out bunkhouse and walked straight to Brannon. "Stuart. Stuart Brannon! Tom Weedin, from Florence. We met a few years back."

"Tom? How are you? What are you doin' up here? What's all this you're writing about me?"

"We've got to stop them. We've got to stop those phony land grant claims right now, Stuart. We've got to stop them right here at Sunrise Creek!"

"Who are these people?"

"Sightseers."

"What do you mean?"

"We've been pumpin' up this standoff pretty strong all across the Territory. We told folks that if they want to know what's really going on, they'd better come down and look at the situation themselves."

"And they did? They all came to watch?"

"Yeah, that's why they're keeping their distance. Amazing, isn't it?"

"Who's in this wagon?" Brannon pointed to the one group that had actually rolled into the yard.

"That's Rugby Jamison, the Surveyor-General!"

Edwin Fletcher came alongside Brannon.

"Edwin, go alert the others. Get Gonzales and Harvey back to the house. Keep them spread out, and don't let anyone infiltrate the buildings. This would be a good scene for the Collectors to try to slip in and take possession." Then he turned to Nelson Barton.

"Mr. Barton, I would like your expertise in this matter."

"Certainly."

Brannon, Barton, and Weedin walked over to the wagon.

"Mr. Jamison? I'm Stuart Brannon."

"Ah, yes, the notorious Stuart Brannon. One can hardly pick up a newspaper without reading of you." He glared at Tom Weedin.

"Where are Judge and Mrs. Quilici?" Brannon asked.

"I believe they made a quick train ride to Yuma. Let me introduce my associate, Mr. Toppington, and these gentlemen are lawyers for the Casa Verde Land Development Corporation, Mr. Stailly and Mr. Greenspan."

"Mr. Brannon, we have come all the way from San Francisco to settle this matter," Greenspan began. "You have caused us considerable consternation and delay by your actions here in Yavapai County."

"Not to mention adverse publicity," Stailly added.

"I caused *you?* I've been shot, fired on by artillery, under siege for two weeks, half my home is burnt up, and three hundred people just moved in on my place—and I caused you consternation?"

"This acreage, as all these people know, does not belong to you, but rather to the Casa Verde Land Development Corporation."

"Gentlemen!" Mr. Jamison intervened. "That's exactly what I came to investigate! We will handle all testimony in an orderly fashion. I have examined the documents, and I will now listen to the claims of both sides. Do you have your attorney with you?"

"Attorney? Well, no . . . but Mr. Barton—"

"Mr. Barton is employed by the federal government just as I am and cannot take sides in this matter."

"I will act as my own attorney."

"Stuart!" Fletcher called. "Up ahead!"

Hank Jedel rode past the carriages and into the yard.

"Get him out of here!" Brannon demanded.

"What? Mr. Jedel? He's a foreman for Casa Verde."

"I don't care if he's the President of the United States. Get him off my place, or I throw him off!"

"Mr. Brannon, we cannot progress with this attitude," Greenspan protested.

Jedel sat in the saddle with his hands resting on the horn. Brannon walked up close to the horse.

"Jedel, get out of this yard immediately!"

"I hardly think you'll be the one givin' orders, Brannon," he taunted.

Suddenly, Brannon grabbed Jedel's vest, and before the man on the horse could draw his gun, he was literally yanked out of the saddle, and he crashed to the ground.

Jedel jumped to his feet, but Brannon's right uppercut sprawled him back to the ground. He went for his holstered revolver, but the toe of Brannon's boot caught his hand and sent the gun flying. Brannon had his own gun out of the holster and shoved it hard underneath Jedel's chin.

"Mister," Brannon panted, "you're leavin' this ranch right now! You have threatened, harassed, and attacked us for the last time!"

Keeping the gun in place, Brannon backed the man out of the yard and shoved him towards the onlookers. Jedel stumbled and fell once more.

Brannon turned and, with his back to Jedel, walked over and rejoined the others. The watching crowd broke into applause and cheers.

"That," shouted Stailly, "is exactly the kind of behavior we are trying to avoid!"

"Then, gentlemen, may I suggest you keep Jedel and his outlaws off my yard."

"And I suggest," Jamison continued, "that this inquiry be held indoors so that such outbursts to attract the attention of the crowd will not happen again."

"I presume Mr. Weedin is invited as an independent witness?"

Jamison nodded approval.

"Well," Brannon conceded, "I cannot offer you the comfort of my home, since the Casa Verde Land Corporation has burnt half of it to the ground. But you may certainly use my barn."

"Is there a table on which we may spread out papers?"

"There's a wagon."

"That will do."

As Jamison, Toppington, and the lawyers carried in several satchels of papers, Brannon barked orders. "Edwin, you come with me inside the barn. Nelson, even though you're not allowed to take sides, I would appreciate your advice."

"Certainly."

"Earl, you and Harvey and Gonzales keep the Collectors out of the yard. No one takes a step towards any building!"

"Yes, sir."

"Stuart?" Reed called.

"Harriet, if you ladies could fix a meal for this group in here, it would be appreciated."

She nodded and scurried towards the house.

It took over two hours for the Casa Verde lawyers to explain their position and Burlingame's claim to the land.

It took Brannon only five minutes to explain his.

"Look, Brannon admits to abandoning the land for two years. We submit to you he only came back to claim it after he knew it belonged to Casa Verde."

"Why would I do that?"

"In order to make a profit. Undoubtedly you thought we would offer you money to leave."

Brannon's cold stare caused the C.V.L. attorney to scoot back to the far side of the wagon.

Then turning to Jamison, Brannon continued. "As you can see from this letter dated June 14, 1876, I was advised by authorities in Prescott that the soil-borne disease that killed my cattle after the flood would be best treated by ceasing to graze the land for at least two years. Following that advice, I took employment elsewhere."

"That was three years ago."

"I was delayed on other matters."

Greenspan spoke up. "Mr. Jamison, how do we know that letter was not forged?"

This time it was Nelson Barton who broke into the conversation. "I can certify that this particular letter has been in my safe for the past three years and that I personally took it out of that safe and handed it and other papers to Mr. Brannon only a few weeks ago."

"And," Fletcher broke in, "I can state that in the two years that I have known Stuart Brannon he has spoke of nothing except returning to this Arizona ranch. I can produce other witnesses who will supply the same information."

"You understand, Mr. Brannon," Jamison continued, "that it is possible for a Spanish land grant, in accordance with the treaty of Guadalupe Hildago, to supersede even the most legitimate claims?"

"Yes, sir, and I'm sure you understand that so-called documents supporting those grants can be purchased in most every town on both sides of the border?"

"Indeed," sighed Jamison, "indeed I do."

"Mr. Brannon?" Earl Howland called from the door. "Miss Harriet has some dinner prepared. She wants to know when you would like it served, and where?"

"Mr. Jamison," Brannon interjected, "would this be a good time for a meal break?"

"I would be delighted."

The entire group moved out into the yard and settled into chairs that had been brought out of the dining room. After serving the others, Harriet Reed came over and sat down next to Brannon.

"How's it going in there?"

"There's more of them."

"What?"

"More people have ridden up, haven't they?"

"Yes, they keep wandering down both roads. It's like going to a—a circus."

"They're coming to see the elephant."

"I don't understand."

"They've heard about gunfights and land feuds all their lives, but most folks have never seen one. So they've come to see one. Like the country farmer that had never seen a circus, they've come to see the elephant."

"Yes, well, you didn't tell me. What happened inside?"

"About two hours of pretty words and legal mumble jumble, and then fifteen minutes of facts."

"Has Jamison come to any conclusions?"

"No—and remember, all he can do is make a recommendation to the Secretary of the Interior."

"Mr. Schurz?"

"Yes, do you know him?"

"Certainly."

"Well, anyway, what I'm saying is that the matter can't be solved in this meeting today. When all these folks go home, we'll still be in the same fix."

"I pray that it will be over before tonight. I, for one, don't believe I could go another night without sleep."

"Yeah, well, keep sending fresh coffee over."

As the men began to reassemble in the barn, Brannon walked over to Howland.

"Earl, are you having any trouble out here?"

"Not yet, Mr. Brannon, but those Collectors seem to have scattered themselves all around the outside of the place. They've mixed in with the crowd. If someone gave a signal and they all moved in at once, we couldn't stop them."

"Help me up on that chair." Brannon let out a yell that startled everyone within shouting distance. "Folks! Thanks for coming! I want to mosey out and visit personally with all of you later on, but we've got this big meetin' going on right now. In the meantime, look around you. There are about fifty gunmen who have been hired to try to take my land away. Now don't jeopardize your safety, but I would appreciate it if you see one of these men start to sneak towards my home, if you'd just tap him on the back of the head with an axe handle and remind him to stay away from my place."

Howland helped him down, and he limped back over to the barn.

Once they all reassembled, it was Jamison's turn to speak. "Gentleman, I want to give you my opinion of this case. I will start first with Mr. Brannon's claim because it's much simpler to deal with. His papers are correct. If there are no previous claims to this land, the ranch is his. There is no case of him either permanently abandoning the land nor proof of wrongful intent to extort money from Casa Verde Development Corporation.

"As for the DePalma-Revera Land Grant claim itself, Mr. Burlingame's lawyers have submitted 106 documents to support their claim. After nine months of consideration and two trips to the archives in Guadalajara and Mexico City, I now give you my conclusion.

"First, of the 106 documents, only 14 address the situation of this particular land grant. The rest are merely background statements and prove nothing whatever about this property.

"Second, 8 of the remaining documents show evidence of having been tampered with. And though they claim to be certified copies, they do not match ones found in Mexican archives. I conclude that they are forgeries. These have mainly to do with tracing the lineage of the De Palma-Revera family.

"Third, I will recommend to the secretary that the remaining 6 documents are forgeries based on the following:

"a. The stylus used to form the letters was metal rather than quill, and therefore they cannot be the age claimed.

"b. There are nine different Spanish words used repeatedly in those pages that didn't come into usage until after Mexican Independence.

"c. The only DePalma-Revera listed in the records of the governor of Santa Fe was a Domingo DePalma-Revera who was apprehended by the governor's troops and shot for leading a rebellion against the Crown. It would hardly seem likely that this same governor would give him one of the largest land grants of all time.

"Therefore, it is my recommendation that the grant be denied."

Greenspan answered with carefully chosen words. "We were aware that coming to this hostile situation would make it almost impossible to get a fair hearing, and we will appeal this recommendation."

"Where does this leave me now?" Brannon asked Jamison.

"The land is yours until proven otherwise."

"And what should I do with these 'Collectors' at my door?"

"That is a matter for the Yavapai County Sheriff, who unfortunately resigned last week."

"Mr. Brannon," Earl Howland interrupted again, "Judge and Mrs. Quilici are here, and they have someone with them."

Brannon limped towards the door. "Before you end this inquiry, I would like to get their report."

"By all means," Jamison agreed as he gathered up his papers.

"Judge!" Brannon called.

"Well, Stuart, I see most of your house is still standing," Sage commented.

"Mr. Jamison, representatives of Casa Verde, Stuart," the judge began, "I would like to introduce to you Miguel LeJandro Alvarez, who has been released into my custody from the Arizona Territorial Prison in Yuma."

"He has bearing on this case?" Jamison asked.

"Indeed. He is serving time for trying to sell fraudulent Spanish land grants in the Yuma area."

"What has this to do with our case?" Greenspan complained.

"First, he has confessed that he sold a box of papers to Warren G. Burlingame in San Diego, California, about fifteen months ago. Second, he says that the papers in the Surveyor-General's possession are identical to the ones I bring you from Yuma, except the name and location of the grant have been altered."

"His testimony won't stand," Stailly protested.

"These documents will." Jamison studied the pages presented to him. Glancing up at Brannon, he noted, "This will never go to Congress. I will recommend in a telegram that the claim be immediately dropped and that those involved in the deception be prosecuted to the fullest extent of the law. You will hear from me within the month. Gentlemen, my work is through here, and I, for one, would much prefer to be in Tucson!"

Tom Weedin, who sat on a sack of oats while he listened to the entire proceedings, hit the barn door running. He informed the crowd of the decision and had his wagon rolling up the hill before Brannon and the others emerged from the barn.

Jubilant cheers rang out as the men exited the barn. The people, who had sat all day and waited, suddenly lost restraint and flooded down into the yard shaking hands, shouting, and laughing.

In the confusion Jamison and the Casa Verde lawyers climbed back into their carriages.

"Mr. Greenspan!" Brannon called through the noise. "Mr. Greenspan!" He hobbled close to the wagon. "Look," he shouted, "where does it go from here? What's Burlingame going to do now?"

"That, of course, is his decision. However, due to the seemingly endless negative publicity over this so-called Yavapai County War, we've been instructed that if the case ruled against us, we're to pay off Mr. Jedel and his men and abandon the Corporation Collection Agency. As of this moment, there are no more Collectors working for Casa Verde."

It was a good hour before the excitement began to calm down. By then it was late in the afternoon. Some of the onlookers had already begun the journey back up the trails both north and south. Others still gathered in the yard and surrounding area.

Brannon found Howland. "What happened to the Collectors?"

"Those San Francisco lawyers paid them off, and most just filtered right out of here. There's a half a dozen up next to the cannon. Mainly it just looks like they're drinkin'. Maybe they're tryin' to figure how to drag it out of here."

"And Jedel?"

"He's up there with them."

By the time the sun began to set, only about thirty gawkers remained at the ranch. They set up camp near Sunrise Creek and decided to wait until the following day to return to their homes.

Fletcher grabbed Brannon by the arm. "Stuart, we've got more visitors."

Two of Jedel's men rode up to the south side of the yard. Brannon limped toward them carrying his Winchester.

"What do you want?" Brannon called.

"Jedel wants to call you out. He says it's time you stopped hiding behind those skirts and faced him straight on."

"Let me get this right. He's got a cannon and six men, and he's calling me a coward?"

"He'll meet you at the creek—just you and him. We'll stay up there on the hill. You can see us from here."

I am not a violent man.

"Tell Jedel he is not worth the bullet or five minutes of my time."

"You backin' out, Brannon?"

The Winchester was at his shoulder and cocked before either man knew what happened.

"Tell him I was not afraid of him when he had fifty men by his side, and I'm certainly not afraid now. If one of you boys wants to try me out, just make a pull for it."

"Wait," one protested. "I ain't drawin' on ya. I ain't whiskey-crazy. It's Jedel."

"He's going to be mad!"

"But he'll be alive. Now," Brannon motioned with the barrel of the rifle, "get off my ranch!"

Howland watched through the spyglass as the two riders drifted back up the hill.

"They're leavin'!" he called.

"All six of them?"

"No, just the two that were down here."

"That leaves four. Sounds almost tame after the past several weeks, doesn't it?"

"We going after them?" Howland inquired.

"Nope. Maybe they'll all be gone by morning."

"Will they come back later on?"

"Only if someone pays them."

"Jedel ain't in it for just pay," Howland cautioned. "I've seen him crazy when he's drunk."

"We'll post a guard and see who's left up there in the morning. If they didn't charge us fifty strong, I doubt if four of them will."

The evening was much quieter than the previous one. Everyone was exhausted from the constant fear and tension. Most were beginning to think about moving on. They still had on their clothes from the night before, but none looked ready for a party.

"I suppose you'll be going on to Phoenix now?" Brannon asked Nelson Barton.

"Well, actually, I've been away from the office so long we have just about decided to return to Prescott."

"When do you have to leave?"

"Tomorrow, if you really think you don't need us here."

Brannon scooted his chair back away from the dining table.

"Are you all going back to Prescott, Miss Cancino?" Brannon pressed.

"Judge and Mrs. Quilici asked me to come stay with them until they go to Phoenix later in the month," Julie announced. "I still want to give that sanitarium a try."

"You will be coming back up to Prescott soon, won't you, Stuart?" Harriet Reed asked.

"Well, there's one thing for sure, I'm going to need to buy a wagonful of lumber to rebuild this place. I suppose you all need to get on the trail first thing in the morning. You'll be able to ride along with the folks down at the creek."

Most of the group made quick exits to get some sleep. Howland helped Miss Cancino to the front porch. Reed and Brannon remained at the table.

"I hope you'll come back to the ranch sometime when it's normal again. I didn't even get to show you around the place."

"I look forward to it."

"Did I ever take you up to the piñon pines?" he asked.

She sighed and tilted her head. "To the graves?"

"Yeah, it's the prettiest place on this entire ranch."

"I would expect it to be. You know, Stuart, most of us will never be quite the same after this siege."

"I don't think the Triple B will stay the same either. It has been real nice to have the rustle of dresses in this house again. I didn't realize how much I missed that."

"Just sit there for a minute and let me clear the table. I think Gwen has collapsed in a corner somewhere."

Brannon felt a soft hand touch his shoulder, and he jerked his head straight up.

"Have I been asleep?" he mumbled.

"Only a short while," Harriet reported. "But that chair doesn't look very comfortable."

"Yeah . . . I think I'll go on out to the barn." He stood, stumbled on his bad foot, and then caught himself on the table.

"Are you all right?"

"Just need a little rest." He hobbled out onto the porch and nodded at Howland and Cancino.

"Earl, nudge me when you turn in, and I'll take a watch. A drunk Jedel is capable of anything."

Within moments Brannon was sound asleep.

At first he thought the explosion was just in a dream—distant, hard to explain, unconnected with his need for rest.

The cannon!

He sat straight up in the straw.

Howland and the other men were pulling themselves to their feet as Brannon dashed for the door.

"What did they shoot at?" he yelled at Fletcher who was leading El Viento out of the corral. "What are you doing with my horse? Where's the spyglass? What did they shoot?"

"It's just Jedel. I guess the others left in the night," Fletcher reported.

"What are you doing with my saddle?"

"Take a look for yourself." Fletcher handed him the spyglass.

"What am I looking for?"

"Your piñon pines."

The pines! He blew up the pines! Lord, no, not Lisa and the baby!

Brannon frantically searched the hillside. Only one pine tree remained, leaning at a forty-five degree angle. The other was a gnarled pile of limbs and roots. For a moment he couldn't take his eyes off the sight. He couldn't speak. Fletcher tightened the cinch, and Brannon yanked himself up into the saddle. Fletcher handed up his Winchester.

"I don't suppose you want me to ride along?"

Brannon kicked El Viento hard, and the horse shot out of the yard and up the hill.

"No . . . I didn't think so." Fletcher sighed.

Harriet Reed ran to his side. "What is it, Edwin?"

"I think—I think Jedel just pushed Brannon over the line."

It's hard to describe all the feelings at that moment. You realize that I had just spent thirty-six hours in that same dress, Lisa's dress, only slept maybe five hours in two days, and then had spent most of the time waiting to get shot or some equally horrid fate.

Well, hearing the explosion, I pulled myself together and ran to the front of the house. I noticed that Mr. Brannon was

horseback and talking with Edwin Fletcher. Since I couldn't
find my shoes, I ran barefoot (yes, Harriet Reed—barefoot!)
over towards them, but Mr. Brannon had sprinted up the hill
before I got there.

That's when Mr. Fletcher, a really charming Englishman,
told me about Jedel blowing up the trees and graves. I just
couldn't believe it. Some acts are so vile they just stagger and
stun one's senses, and that's how I felt. I must admit I pulled
the spyglass right out of Mr. Fletcher's hand.

Oh, you must get a sense of the scene. It is barely dawn—
the mountains are still fairly green, the creek splits the valley, the empty sky is grayish-blue, a gentle but cool breeze
floats across the yard. There's the smell of horses, and ashes,
and men.

In the scope I see a black horse—a big, very fast black
horse galloping up the distant hill. Mr. Brannon's hat is flap-
ping on his back, held on by the stampede string. His rifle is
in his right hand, and he is wildly spurring the horse. Then
I move the spyglass up the hill and see the cannon and a man
furiously working to reload. I almost fainted when it dawned
on me that the cannon was now pointed right at Mr.
Brannon. He would literally be blown right out of this
world!

From that distance an interesting phenomenon occurs.
You see the smoke from the cannon firing long before you
hear the report of the explosion. Well, the smoke flew. Then
came the horrible sound of the explosion. My heart sank, but
I looked back, and Mr. Brannon was still galloping up the
mountain.

As we learned later, the old cannon, still hot from the first
shot, misfired and literally blew up. All I could see was
Brannon riding into a cloud of smoke. Then we heard three
shots being fired, and finally I saw him, still mounted, race
across the hill to the little cemetery.

I was informed by Mr. Howland that what we heard were
shots from a handgun, and Mr. Brannon had only carried his
rifle with him.

Mr. Fletcher, Mr. Howland, and I mounted up as soon as

we could (no, I did not ride sidesaddle) and made our way up the hill. The cannon was split on one side, and Mr. Jedel lay about twelve feet away. Mr. Howland and Mr. Fletcher dismounted and proclaimed Mr. Jedel dead. It seems a piece of the cannon had hit him in the stomach, but he had time to fire three bullets at Mr. Brannon, who, as it turned out, escaped with only a hole in his hat.

Well, I started to ride on over to the grave sites, but Mr. Fletcher wouldn't let me. I was as angry as a schoolgirl at the time, but looking back, I know he, as usual, was quite correct.

It was early afternoon before Mr. Brannon returned to the house. Most of the crowd at the creek had begun their journey home. Julie had left with Judge and Mrs. Quilici about midmorning. We had our carriages ready to depart and only waited to say good-bye to our host.

He didn't speak to a soul until after he put the horse in the corral. I ran to him in the middle of the yard, and he put his calloused hands on my shoulders, touching the rose dress that had once been his Lisa's. I don't know if I can do justice to this scene, but his eyes told the whole story.

They were old.

Red.

Tired.

Sad.

And they belonged only to her.

I wanted to hold him in my arms and rock his deep hurts away, but the best I could do was drop my head and begin to cry. We stood there without speaking for a few minutes. Then the others were loaded and ready to leave. There was nothing any of us could think of to say.

He looked up at me in the carriage and sighed. "Harriet, I didn't shoot Jedel. I am not a violent man."

I truly want to believe him.

To say the past several days since the Yavapai County War have been uneventful would be an understatement. After being around Mr. Brannon, I have a distinct feeling that all of life will be rather dull. I would be bored silly if I didn't have my novel to work on and you to write to.

Mr. Fletcher did send word that he and Mr. Howland will be coming to Prescott next week to purchase a load of lumber. It will be like a wonderful little reunion to see them again.

I did tell you that Mr. Fletcher is an Earl or Lord or something, didn't I?

Give my best to Rachel.

> Affectionately yours,
> Miss Harriet Reed